"You really do think someone wants to harm me?" Natalie asked. **"That it's not my imagination?"**

"Isn't that why you hired me?" Clint asked.

She stared into Clint's dark eyes and pressed a hand over her mouth to hide the way her lips trembled. Yes. But why would anyone want to harm her?

Those dark whispers she had tried so hard to close out just before she drifted off to sleep each night these past eight or so weeks nudged her now, echoing deep in her mind. She closed her eyes and let them come. Laughter, soft, feminine... Then the raised voices—a man and a woman. Was it a real memory? Something from before her fall? Something from childhood?

She waited until Clint had parked in front of her home to say, "I don't intend to stay holed up in this house. I can't...do that."

He put his hand on her arm. "Wherever you go, I go."

Dear Reader,

I am so pleased to bring you *Dark Whispers*, a new beginning for my Faces of Evil series for Harlequin Intrigue. The characters are very close to my heart, and I am certain you will enjoy following former FBI profiler Jess Harris Burnett as her private investigation agency reveals evil that lurks behind the seemingly ordinary. Next month be sure to look for *Still Waters*. And there will be more to come!

Harlequin Intrigue has been my home for nearly two decades and I am so excited to continue being a part of this amazing family. So many of you write to me and I appreciate every letter! Keep them coming. Along with the Faces of Evil series, Harlequin Intrigue and I will be bringing you more Colby Agency stories in the future. Look for Colby Agency: The Next Generation soon! It's hard to believe but Victoria's granddaughter, Jamie, is all grown up and ready to follow in her grandmother's footsteps.

I have more exciting news. My new most chilling series yet, Shades of Death from MIRA Books, is coming in the spring of 2017, starting with *No Darker Place*. But be sure to pick up the ebook prequel, *The Blackest Crimson*, to get the terrifying backstory.

You can follow me at www.debrawebb.com and sign up for my newsletter for news about my latest releases.

Best,

Deb

DARK
WHISPERS

USA TODAY Bestselling Author
DEBRA WEBB

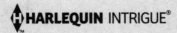

I have met many people in this life but few have proved to be
so dear to me as the wonderful Marijane Diodati. Thank you,
my friend, for caring so very much for me and for my stories.
I will cherish you always.

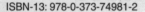

ISBN-13: 978-0-373-74981-2

Dark Whispers

Copyright © 2016 by Debra Webb

Recycling programs
for this product may
not exist in your area.

This edition published by arrangement with Harlequin Books S.A.

For questions and comments about the quality of this book,
please contact us at CustomerService@Harlequin.com.

Printed in U.S.A.

www.Harlequin.com

Debra Webb is the award-winning *USA TODAY* bestselling author of more than one hundred novels, including reader favorites the Faces of Evil, the Colby Agency and the Shades of Death series. With more than four million books sold in numerous languages and countries, Debra's love of storytelling goes back to childhood on a farm in Alabama. Visit Debra at www.debrawebb.com.

Visit the Author Profile page at Harlequin.com for more titles.

CAST OF CHARACTERS

Clint Hayes—A former homicide detective and the most experienced investigator on Jess's new team. Clint is certain he can help Natalie, but he has a few dark secrets of his own.

Natalie Drummond—Natalie suffered a traumatic brain injury two years ago and now she's trying to get her life back together...only dark whispers and equally dark secrets from the past keep haunting her.

Jess Harris Burnett—Former FBI profiler and deputy chief of major crimes. Jess has joined forces with her old friend Buddy Corlew in a private investigation agency in an effort to help victims of crimes the police can't always resolve.

April Drummond Keating—Natalie's sister wants to help, but is she hiding too many secrets of her own?

David Keating—Natalie's brother-in-law is far too focused on running for office to worry that she might be in danger.

Heath Drummond—Natalie fears her brother believes she might be losing her mind.

Vince Farago—He was supposed to be Natalie's friend, but was he really only out to get ahead of her at the firm?

Mike Beckett—How long has he been watching Natalie, and for whom?

Art Rosen—The partner at the firm Natalie considered a friend and mentor. Was she wrong all those years?

Lori Wells, Chet Harper, Chad Cook—Detectives from Jess's former major crimes team who give her a hand whenever the need arises.

Dan Burnett—Birmingham's chief of police and Jess's husband.

Chapter One

4th Avenue North
Birmingham, Alabama
Monday, September 19, 3:30 p.m.

Former Deputy Chief Jess Harris Burnett repositioned the nameplate on the new *old* desk in the center of her small office. A matching credenza stood against the wall beneath the window. She had a nice view of the street, unlike her partner whose office window overlooked the not-so-attractive alley at the back of their downtown historic building. She'd offered to toss a coin, but he'd insisted she take the nicer view. Buddy Corlew, her old friend turned business partner, actually preferred the office with the potential *backdoor* escape route. He boasted that he'd worked sufficient cheating spouse cases to appreciate the option of a hasty retreat.

Jess sighed as she surveyed her new office

space. A couple of bookcases lined the wall to the right of her desk, while framed accomplishments and accolades dotted the left. Her new office didn't look half bad now that everything was in place. The lingering doubt about the big career change was gone for the most part as were the rumors in the media and even in the department. The people she cared about understood and supported her reasons for change. Though she missed her major crimes team and, to some degree, working in the field, family and friends were what mattered most to her now.

Her closest friends, Detective Lori Wells and Dr. Sylvia Baron, had helped Jess with the decorating as well as the furnishing of the offices. Since the building was one of Birmingham's oldest, they had chosen to go with a casual vintage decor. Jess arranged the two mismatched chairs in front of her desk and stood back to have a look. "Not bad at all."

The baby kicked hard and she jumped. Smiling, Jess rubbed her belly. Her husband Dan insisted this child would play football at the University of Alabama just like his grandfather had back in the day. Jess shook her head. She had no desire to plan her unborn child's college career just yet, much less whether or not he would participate in such a brutal sport. But then, this was Alabama—football was practically a religion.

She supposed the idea was no different than her mother-in-law, Katherine, already having Bea, their eighteen-month-old daughter, enrolled in ballet class and baby yoga.

Jess sighed. Her sister, Lily, had warned her that motherhood came with a whole host of new obligations, expectations and no shortage of worries. "And here you are going for round two, Jessie Lee." She rested a hand on her heavy belly. As frustrating and terrifying as being a parent could be, she wouldn't trade it for anything. She wondered if their baby boy would have dark hair and blue eyes like his father? Their little girl had Jess's blond hair and brown eyes.

A bell tinkled in the lobby and Jess wandered out of her office and toward the sound. The private investigation agency she and her old high school friend Buddy Corlew had decided to establish opened on Wednesday with an open house scheduled for next Monday. Had Buddy decided to drop back by or had she left the front door unlocked? Her pulse rate climbed with every step she took toward the entry. She'd spent too many years analyzing and helping to apprehend serial killers to ignore the potential for trouble. Memories of last spring's ordeal with Ted Holmes attempted to emerge but she suppressed them. That nightmare was over. *Don't look back.*

Buddy stood in the lobby appraising the work

Jess and her friends had done. She relaxed. "I didn't think you were coming back today."

"Sylvia told me you were still here." Buddy glanced around the lobby and nodded his approval. "Looks great, kid."

Buddy was the only person in the world who had ever called her kid. The fact that he still did reminded her that in many ways he would forever be living in the past. His music taste was pre-1990, his long hair was fastened in a ponytail, and he still strutted around in worn denim and scarred leather the same way he had in high school. Enough said.

"Great might be an overstatement," Jess surveyed the lobby, "but at least we won't be scaring off clients." The exposed brick walls and concrete floors looked less like a dungeon with a few carefully placed upholstered chairs and a couple of tasteful pieces of secondhand art purchased at the most recent fundraiser Dan's mother hosted.

"Did you get your office squared away?"

"I did." Jess braced a hand on her hip and ignored the ache that had started in her lower back. She'd certainly overdone it today. "I was about to call it a day."

Buddy glanced at her round belly and smiled. "I can't wait until Sylvia actually looks pregnant." As hard as it was to believe, Buddy and Sylvia, Jefferson County's medical examiner and the daughter of one of Birmingham's old money families, had married and were now expecting a child.

Jess and Buddy had grown up on the not-so-appealing side of Birmingham and somehow they'd both managed to do okay. Jess had spent most of her law enforcement career with the FBI, first as a field agent and then as a profiler. Just over two years ago she had returned to Birmingham and started a new career with Birmingham PD as deputy chief of Major Crimes. After twenty years separated by their careers and geography, she'd married her high school sweetheart, Daniel Burnett, the chief of police.

Buddy's life had taken a somewhat less direct route to where they were now. A womanizing rebel in high school, he'd ended up spending a tour of duty in the military right out of high school to avoid trouble with the law. Later, several years as a BPD cop and then a detective had ended on a bit of a sour note. Buddy, however, being Buddy, had bounced back. He'd opened a small private investigation shop and done well. Falling for and marrying Sylvia had changed the man as nothing else could have. He could not wait to be a daddy. The change left a large portion of Birmingham's female population bemoaning the loss.

"Don't worry," Jess assured him, "that will

happen soon enough." She suspected her old friend didn't have a clue what he was in for. Sylvia would ensure Buddy suffered every moment of discomfort she endured for the next several months.

The bell over the door tinkled again. Jess turned as Clint Hayes strolled in, a box under one arm and a briefcase in his hand. Clint had been a member of Jess's BPD major crimes team. He'd asked if he might come onboard at B&C Investigations when Jess first announced she was leaving the department. She hadn't been able to deny that having an investigator with a law degree as well as several years as a detective under his belt was attractive. No matter, she had discussed the idea with Dan before acting on Clint's request. He had a right to know one of his detectives was considering making the move with her. Dan had been so glad Jess was leaving police work behind, he'd been only too happy to see Clint go with her. That he was handsome and dressed impeccably wouldn't hurt, either.

"I cleaned out my desk at the department," Clint announced in greeting. "I thought I'd get settled here."

Buddy clapped him on the back. "Glad to have you, Hayes."

"We've set up several desks in the large office at the end of the hall," Jess explained. She and

Buddy had taken the two smaller offices. The larger one would allow for several investigators to share the space. A third smaller office would serve as a conference space for meeting with clients. Closer to the lobby was a tiny kitchenette with a narrow hall to the only bathroom and a rear exit. "Take your pick."

"Just like old times." Clint flashed Jess a grin and headed that way. Buddy followed, filling him in on the open house planned for a week from today.

For now, Clint was their only investigator. Buddy was working on recruiting. They had interviewed three others so far. Their secretary, Rebecca Scott, who would also serve as a receptionist and occasionally as a babysitter when Lily and Katherine were tied up, was scheduled to start tomorrow. Jess was immensely grateful to find someone willing to wear so many hats and whom she trusted with her child while she met with clients and assigned investigators.

Assessing cases and determining the best way to proceed wouldn't be that different from her profiler days—other than the fact that they wouldn't likely be tracking serial killers and hunting murderers. Then again, throughout her career she always seemed to have a penchant for attracting the faces of evil.

The bell over the door jingled again, drawing

Jess from the memory of one serial killer in particular. Four and a half months ago Ted Holmes had done all within his power to reach the highest level of evil by resurrecting the persona of Eric Spears and reenacting his obsession with Jess.

Banishing the memories once more, Jess produced a smile for the woman, thirty or so, who stood just inside the door as if she couldn't decide what to do next. She was petite, around Jess's height of five-four. Her black hair was long and lush; she was attractive. Her manner of dress, a soft beige pencil skirt with matching jacket and heels, suggested a career woman. Her gaze moved around the lobby, eventually landing on Jess. The fear and hesitation in her expression gave Jess pause.

"I need a private investigator," she said, her voice trembling the slightest bit.

Jess was on the verge of telling her they didn't open until the day after tomorrow when the woman added, "I shot a man."

When she swayed, Jess hurried to usher her into the nearest chair. "Why don't you have a seat? I'll get you a bottle of water."

Their first potential client shook her head. "No. Please." She put her hand on Jess's arm. "I need help."

"Let's start with your name." Jess settled into

a seat on the opposite side of the reclaimed factory cart that served as a coffee table.

"Natalie Drummond."

"Well, Ms. Drummond, it sounds as if you might need the police rather than our services. I'll be happy to call someone for you." Jess's first thought was to call Lori. Detective Lori Wells now worked in the Crimes Against Persons division. Jess considered her a dear friend and she was one of the best detectives in the department. It didn't hurt that Lori's husband, Chet Harper, was the ranking detective in the BPD's major crimes team—as well as a good friend.

Drummond shook her head. "You don't understand. I did call the police, but they can't help me."

The woman looked sincere and certainly terrified, but her story didn't quite make sense. "I'm not sure I'm following you. Why can't the police help you?"

Drummond wrung her hands in her lap. "The man I shot is missing. They found no evidence of an intruder in my home…even the gun I used was missing." She shook her head, tears bright in her eyes. "I don't understand how that's possible. I shot him." She looked straight at Jess. "I know I shot him. He fell to the floor. He…he was bleeding. I ran out of the house and waited for the police to arrive." Her eyebrows drew together in a worried frown. "When they arrived he was gone."

"Can you remember the detective's name who came to the scene?" Whatever happened, Ms. Drummond was visibly shaken. That level of fear wasn't easily manufactured.

"Lieutenant Grady Russell."

Jess was acquainted with Russell. He was a detective in the Crimes Against Persons division. Russell was a good cop. "Why don't I give the lieutenant a call and see what I can find out?"

Drummond nodded, visibly relieved. "Thank you."

Jess stood. "Come with me and I'll introduce you to one of our investigators." No reason to mention that he was their only investigator.

Buddy was in his office on the phone as they passed. Jess escorted Drummond to the end of the hall where Clint was organizing his desk.

"Clint, this is Natalie Drummond."

"Ms. Drummond." Clint gifted her with a nod.

"Ms. Drummond will explain her situation to you while I make a call to Lieutenant Russell."

Clint invited Drummond to have a seat. Rather than go to her office, Jess went to Buddy's and closed the door. When he'd ended his call, she said, "We need a conference call with Russell about our first client. She says she shot a man who is now missing."

Buddy raised his eyebrows as he set the phone to speaker and made the call. "You always did attract the strange ones."

He needn't remind her.

Three rings and Russell answered. Jess quickly explained the situation and asked for any insights the lieutenant could provide.

"We received the call early this morning," Russell confirmed. "I have to tell you, I think maybe the lady is a little wrong in the head."

Jess was immensely grateful for the thick brick walls of the historic building that helped ensure privacy between offices. "What does that mean, Lieutenant?" If the man said Drummond was hormonal or flighty, Jess might just walk the few blocks to the Birmingham Police Department and kick his butt on principal.

"About two years ago Natalie Drummond had a fall down the stairs of that mansion her daddy left her. She was banged up pretty good, but it was the brain injury that left her with big problems. According to her family, she still suffers with the occasional memory lapse and reasoning issue."

"She had a traumatic brain injury?" Jess frowned and rubbed at the resulting lines spanning her forehead. Even two years later, an injury like that could explain Drummond's uncertainty as to the sequence of recent events.

"That's the story according to her brother, Heath Drummond," Russell confirmed.

Now there was a name Jess recognized. "As in Drummond Industries?"

"The one and only," Russell confirmed. "The brother says she hasn't been the same since the fall. She spent months in rehab. He thinks maybe she's having some kind of relapse. About two months ago, she started insisting that someone was coming into her house at night. Every time she told the story it was a little different. The brother decided she was hallucinating. Apparently that can happen with TBIs. This morning she called 9-1-1 and claimed she'd shot a man. We arrive and there's no body. No blood. No signs of an altercation. Nothing. There was no weapon found on the premises, yet she swears she discharged a .38 at an intruder. She also swears she left him bleeding on the floor."

Jess exchanged a look with Buddy.

"You believe she imagined the whole thing," Buddy said.

"At this point, yeah, that's the only explanation that makes sense."

"Thanks so much, Lieutenant." Before ending the call, Jess assured him she would pass along any information she might discover relevant to the case. To Buddy she said, "Whether she shot anyone or not, it sounds as if Ms. Drummond needs our help."

"I guess we have our first case." Buddy came around to the front of his desk and offered his hand. "I'll leave the logistics to you. I have another investigator to interview over at Cappy's."

Jess took his hand and struggled to her feet. Cappy's Corner Grill was a cop hangout over on 29th that served the best burgers in town. Local cops, private investigators and bounty hunters frequently used Cappy's for unofficial staff meetings.

"Clint is the right investigator for this one," Jess said, the wheels inside her head already turning. She remembered well how cocky the detective had been when he'd first joined her major crimes team, but time had softened his hard edges.

Buddy shot her a wink as they exited his office. "Good thing, since he's our only investigator."

"True." Jess turned to the office at the end of the hall where Clint was interviewing their first client. Whatever troubles Natalie Drummond faced, real or imagined, Jess would see that she received the help she needed.

No one should have to fight her demons alone.

Chapter Two

Clint pulled into the driveway behind Natalie Drummond. He surveyed the place she called home and blew out a long, low whistle. If the lady lived here—the estate looked more like a castle than a home—then she was loaded. He should have realized she was related to *the* Drummonds of Birmingham.

He climbed out of his Audi and strolled up to her BMW as she opened the door. When she emerged her lips tilted the slightest bit with a shaky smile. "I appreciate you being able to start right away. I was afraid it would be days or even weeks before I could retain the services I needed."

"I'll work as quickly as possible to get to the bottom of the trouble, Ms. Drummond. No one should be afraid in their own home." Even if it was large enough to host the next governor's summit.

"You should call me Natalie." She exhaled a big breath and sent a worried glance back at the street.

"Natalie," he repeated. "As long as you call me Clint."

She nodded, and then led the way to the front door. When she fished the keys from her bag, he reached for them. "Why don't I go in first?"

Obviously relieved, she turned over the keys.

As he opened the door the first detail he noted was the lack of a warning from the security system. "You don't arm your system when you leave the house?"

"With all that happened this morning, I suppose I forgot." She closed her eyes and shook her head. "Like I said, I didn't go back in the house after the police left. I couldn't."

He handed the keys back to her, placed a hand at the small of her back and ushered her across the threshold. He surveyed the entry hall. The ceiling soared high above a grand balcony on the second floor. A large painting hung on the broad expanse of wall that flanked the ornate staircase. He recognized Natalie as a child of around ten or twelve in the painting.

"My family," she said, following his gaze. "My

parents are both gone now. There's my younger sister, April, and my older brother, Heath. Heath runs the family business and April is a trophy wife who specializes in fund-raising." She said the last with something less than pride as she placed her purse and keys on a table near the door. "The kitchen is on the right at the end of the hall. That's where…it happened."

Clint hesitated, the sticky notes on the mirror above the hall table snagging his attention. There were several yellow notes and one pink one. *Leave the keys and your purse here. Lock the door. Arm the security system.* The pink note read *Check the peephole before opening the door.*

"I don't need them as much as I used to," she said with a noticeable resignation in her tone. "My short-term memory gets better every day." She locked the door. "It's certain parts of my long-term memory that still have a few too many holes."

He gestured to the notes. "This was part of the process of getting back into your normal routine?"

She nodded. "I'm not sure anything about my routine will ever be called normal again, but I manage."

"I imagine the journey has been a challenging one." Clint moved toward the kitchen. "Back at the office you said your sister spent a great deal of time helping you get back on your feet?"

"She stayed with me every night for the first year. When she wasn't with me there was a nurse." A weary sigh escaped her lips. "For ten months I was fine on my own, and then...the voices started. April stays the night whenever I need her despite my brother-in-law's insistence that he needs his wife at home."

"Your brother-in-law is...?"

"David Keating, the son of Birmingham's new mayor, who sees himself as governor one day. He's running for state representative and insists that April should be at his side at all times. You haven't seen the billboards plastered all over the city? Vote for Truth and Family Values." Natalie shook her head. "Personally, I believe he's worried that I'm losing my mind and he doesn't want his wife too close to anything unpleasant that might end up attached to his name in the news." She paused. "Sorry. I'm being unkind. In truth, David has been very thoughtful since the fall. Forgive me if I'm a little too blunt at times."

"No apology necessary. Do you and your siblings get along?"

"As well as any I suppose." Her heels clicked on the marble floor as they continued toward the kitchen. "Five years ago, after our father died, I think people expected there to be dissention, but we all felt the terms of the will were remarkably well thought out. Heath inherited the family business, which made perfect sense since he was the only one with any interest in overseeing it. He was Father's right hand. I inherited the house and April was endowed with the largest portion of the family financial trust. Father was well aware of my younger sister's love of spending. The trust pays out slowly over her life so there's no fear of her ever being destitute in the event her marriage to David doesn't work out."

They reached the wide arched entrance to the kitchen and Clint paused. "You're an attorney?"

She stared at the sleek tile floor. "I was. It remains to be seen if I will be again. I feel more like an assistant now. Two years ago I was up for partner at Brenner, Rosen and Taylor. I would have been the youngest partner in the firm's history. Most of the past two years I've been on extended disability leave. I returned to work a few weeks ago. I review other people's cases to see if we're doing all we can for each client. I'm certain the partners fear that giving me a case of my own at this point would be premature, perhaps even detrimental to the firm's reputation. After what happened this morning, who can blame them?"

Her work history was impressive. Brenner,

Rosen and Taylor was a small but very prestigious law firm. "Why don't you walk me through exactly what happened this morning."

Natalie drew in a deep breath and squared her shoulders. "I was preparing to go to the office. The security system was apparently unarmed. I could've sworn I set it before I went to bed, but evidently I didn't." She sighed and rubbed at her temple as if a headache had begun there. "I still forget things sometimes and get things out of order, but those instances rarely happen anymore—at least that's what I thought."

"What time did you get up?" Clint moved to the back door. According to the police report, Natalie believed the alleged intruder entered the kitchen through the door leading from the gardens and patio since it had been standing open. All other entry points had been locked when the police arrived, seemingly confirming her allegation. Clint opened the door and crouched down to have a look at the lock and the knob.

"At six," she said in answer to his question. "I remember because the grandfather clock in the entry hall started to chime the hour. It's a habit of mine to count the chimes." She looked away as if the admission embarrassed her. "I've done it since I was a child."

Clint smiled, hoping to help her relax. "I count buttons. Whenever I button my shirt, I count."

Her strained expression softened a bit at his confession. "I guess we all have our eccentricities."

Focusing on his examination of the door, he saw no indication of forced entry. Back at the office, he'd sent a text to Lori Wells requesting a copy of the police report. A quick perusal of the report she'd immediately emailed him had showed the same findings. Clint hadn't really expected to find anything. Still, a second look never hurt. He pushed to his feet. "You were upstairs when you heard an intruder?"

She nodded. "I was dressed and ready to go when I heard a noise down here."

"Describe the noise for me."

She considered the question for a moment. "There was a lot of banging as if whoever was down here was searching for something."

The evidence techs had dusted for prints, but hadn't found any usable ones except Natalie's, which meant the intruder wore gloves and that she had a very dedicated and thorough cleaning staff. Most surfaces in any home were littered with prints. "You came down the stairs," Clint prompted.

"First I came to the landing. I thought maybe Suzanna, my housekeeper, had arrived early." She hugged her arms around herself as if the memories stole the warmth from her body. "I saw him standing at the bottom of the stairs, but I couldn't see his entire face. He was wearing a mask. Like a ski mask where all you can see are the eyes and across the bridge of the nose. I ran back to my room and grabbed my cell phone and my father's handgun from the nightstand. When I came down the stairs I didn't see him anymore. The back door was open so I assumed he'd fled." She took a deep breath. "I came into the kitchen to close the door and suddenly I heard him breathing… behind me. It was as if he'd been waiting for me to come."

"Did he touch you?"

She shook her head. "I spun around and fired the weapon."

Clint closed and locked the back door. "You're certain the intruder was male."

The sound of the door locking or maybe the question snapped her from the silence she'd drifted into. She flinched. "Absolutely. He was tall and strong and he had a scar." She pointed to the spot between her eyebrows.

"He never spoke?"

She shook her head. "He staggered back and then fell to the floor. There was blood on his shirt."

"You ran outside to wait for the police?"

She nodded. "I dropped the gun and ran. I was confused. That still happens when I get overexcited or upset and, quite frankly, I was terrified."

Clint would ask her more about the traumatic brain injury later. According to the police report there was no indication of foul play in the home and no gun was found. Since the detective at the scene had decided the whole event was Drummond's imagination, no test for gunshot residue had been performed. "Did blood splatter on your clothes or your shoes?"

She frowned. "No." Her head moved from side to side. "I suppose there should have been." She closed her eyes for a moment before continuing. "I know what I saw. There was a man here. He wore a black ski mask. I fired the weapon, the sound still echoes inside me whenever I think of that moment."

"You believe," he offered, "while you were waiting for the police the intruder fled, taking the gun with him."

"Yes."

CLINT HAYES DID not believe her.

Natalie didn't have to wonder. She saw the truth in his eyes. There was no evidence to support her story. Nothing. Her brain injury made her an unreliable witness at best. How could she expect anyone to believe her?

Maybe she was losing her mind. Her own brother thought she was imagining things.

"Let's talk about why someone would want to create a situation like the one that played out in your home this morning."

Hope dared to bloom in her chest. "Are you saying you believe me?"

"Yes." He nodded. "I do."

Startled, Natalie fought to gather her wits. She had hoped to find someone who would believe her. Now that she had, she felt weak with relief and overwhelmed with gratitude. "Would you like coffee or tea?"

"No thank you, but don't let me stop you."

"I don't drink coffee after the middle of the afternoon for fear I won't sleep." Her life was quite sad now. What would this handsome, obviously intelligent man think if he knew just how sad? What difference did money and position matter in the end? Very little, she had learned. The years of hard work to reach the pinnacle of her field meant nothing now. She could no more battle an opponent in the courtroom than a ten-year-old could hope to win a presidential debate.

All she had been or ever hoped to be was either gone or broken. Her mother had warned her all-work-and-no-play attitude would come back to haunt her one day. *What kind of life will you have without someone to share it with?* Her mother's words reverberated through her.

A lonely one, Mother. Very lonely.

"Are you taking medication?"

"I have a number of medications, Mr. Hayes." She led the way to an enormous great room where her family had hosted the Who's Who of Birmingham. "There are ones for anxiety and others for sleep—all to be taken as needed. So far I've done all right without them more than six months. I take over-the-counter pain relievers for the headaches that have become fewer and further between."

She settled into her favorite chair. Mr. Hayes took a seat across the coffee table from her. The idea that he might not actually believe her but needed to pad the company's bottom line crossed her mind. The other three agencies she'd contacted this afternoon weren't interested in taking her case. What made this one different? She'd stumbled upon B&C Investigations completely by accident. She'd walked away from the third rejection and noticed the new sign in the window on the way to her car.

"Do you have any personal enemies that you know of?"

She shook her head. "No family issues. No work issues. I can't imagine anyone who would want to do this. Why break into my home? Nothing appears to be missing."

"Let's talk about the people closest to you."

"My sister and I have always made it a point to have dinner a couple of times a week. Since the fall, she stays the night whenever I need her—or when she decides it's necessary. I don't see my brother as often. He's very busy. There's Suzanna Clark, the housekeeper, and her husband, Leonard, the gardener."

"You said your sister started staying with you at night again because of the voices."

Natalie hated admitting this part, but it was necessary. "About two months ago I started waking up at night and hearing voices—as if someone is in the house. I get up and search every room only to find I'm here alone." If only she could convey how very real the voices sounded. It terrified her that perhaps her brother was right and she was imagining them. "Until this morning."

"What about your colleagues at the office?"

The uneasiness that plagued her when she thought of work seeped into her bones. Since the fall, her professional inadequacy filled her with dread whenever the subject of work came up. She'd once lived for her career.

"I have my assistant, Carol. Art Rosen is the partner I work closest with. I'm well acquainted with everyone on staff. I have no rivals or issues with my colleagues, if that's what you're asking."

"Friends or a boyfriend?"

Ah, now he would learn the truly saddest part. "Before the injury, I had lots of friends, most were associated with work. We lost touch during my recovery." She forced a smile. "There's nothing like tragedy to send the people you thought were your friends running in the other direction. It was partly my fault. I was always so strong and self-reliant. People didn't want to see the weak, needy me. Except for Sadie. She's my psychologist as well as my friend."

"Boyfriend?" he repeated. "Fiancé?"

She drew in a big breath. "There was a boyfriend. He had asked me to marry him but I kept putting him off. Work was my top priority. About three months into my recovery, he apparently no longer had the stomach for who I'd become."

The dark expression on the investigator's face told her exactly what he thought about such a man.

Natalie shook her head. "Don't blame him, Mr. Hayes. I'm—"

"Clint," he reminded her.

"Clint," she acknowledged.

"If he cared enough to propose," Clint argued, "there's no excuse for his inability to see you through a difficult time."

"He proposed to the woman I used to be." Natalie understood the reasons all too well. Steven Vaughn had ambitious plans that didn't include a potentially disabled wife. "I'm not that person anymore. I doubt I ever will be. Part of me was lost to the injury and now my entire life is different. I don't blame him for not wanting to be a part of it. After all, if you invest in gold, silver is not a suitable substitution."

Clint studied her for a long moment before going on. "No one in your circle would have had reason to want to do you harm at the time of your accident or now?"

Natalie laughed, a self-deprecating sound. "Therein lies the true rub. Though my current short-term memory works well now, everything beyond six months ago is a very different story. So I can't answer that question because I can't remember. To my knowledge I have no enemies. My colleagues and family know of no one who gave me any real trouble in the past."

"How much of your memory did you lose?"

"Perhaps the better word is *misplaced*. The injury jumbled things up. Our lives—our memories—are stored. Like files in a filing cabinet. Imagine if that cabinet was turned upside down, the drawers would open and those files would spill all over the floor. The contents of the files are still there, but they're hard to retrieve because now they're out of order."

"So you do remember things."

She nodded. "Yes. As my brain healed from the injury, it was like starting over. I had to relearn how to communicate, how to function, mentally as well as physically. As my vocabulary returned, I used the wrong words like saying *hands* when I meant *gloves* or *feet* when I meant *shoes*. Memories came in disorderly fragments. Most often they returned when prompted by some activity or person. It's difficult to say what I've lost when I have no idea what I had. My sister and brother remind me of childhood events and then I recall them vividly. I can look at photographs and recall almost instantly what happened. So, I suppose I've temporarily lost many things. But, so far, the memories return when triggered."

"Then someone may have caused your accident two years ago and you just don't remember."

The dark foreboding that always appeared when she spoke of the fall pressed in on her even as she shook her head. "No. I was here with my sister. There was no one else in the house. My sister and I have been over the details of that night numerous times. If you're suggesting that someone pushed me down the stairs, that isn't what happened."

"All right then, we'll focus our investigation on life since the accident."

She wanted to nod and say that was the proper course of action and yet some feeling or instinct she couldn't name urged her to look back for something she had missed. Frustration had her pushing the idea away. The hardest part of her new reality was not being able to trust her own brain to guide her 100 percent of the time. She also wanted to correct his use of *accident*. She had never been able to see what happened that way. To Natalie it was the *fall*—a moment in time that changed her life forever. A part of her wondered if her inability to see it as an accident was her mind trying to tell her something she needed to remember.

"Since you only recently returned to work, has there been a particular case that may be the root of this new trouble? Maybe someone believes they can scare you into some sort of cooperation."

"I somehow doubt that giving my two cents' worth, so to speak, on the steps that have been missed or that should be taken on other people's cases would garner that sort of attention. Considering what happened today, I doubt I'll have a position at the firm much longer."

Natalie decided that was the part that hurt the most. Losing her friends and even her so-called soul mate hadn't been the end of the world. It was losing her ability to practice law that devastated her completely. Work was the one thing that had never let her down. Being an attorney had defined her.

What did she have now?

This big old house and…not much else.

Her attention settled on the investigator watching her so closely. She hoped he could find something to explain how the man she shot suddenly disappeared other than the possibility that she really was losing her mind.

Chapter Three

Clint's first client as a private detective had been at work for an hour when he decided to make his appearance at the offices of Brenner, Rosen and Taylor.

He'd stayed with Natalie last night until her sister, April, arrived. He'd gone home afterward and done some research on Natalie's career and background. He'd discovered that one of the senior associates at Natalie's firm was Vince Farago, an old school pal of his from Samford. Clint gritted his teeth. He wondered if Natalie was aware that the man could not be trusted in any capacity. Farago was the proverbial snake in the grass.

Clint would stop at Natalie's office and check in with her after he visited with his old *friend*.

He had a few questions for Farago, and frankly he intended to enjoy watching the guy squirm.

The moment he entered the posh lobby the receptionist looked up. "Good morning, sir, how may I help you?"

Another receptionist manned the ringing phones, ensuring someone was always available to greet arriving clients. The building spanned from 6th to 29th, filling the corner of the busy intersection much like New York's Flatiron building. The lobby's glass walls looked out over the hectic pace of downtown Birmingham.

"Clint Hayes," he said. "I need a moment of Mr. Farago's time this morning."

The receptionist made a sad face. "I'm so sorry, Mr. Hayes, but Mr. Farago is completely booked today. May I set up something for you later in the week?"

Clint gave his head a shake. "Let him know I'm here. I trust he'll be able to spare a minute or two." For old time's sake, he opted not to add.

The receptionist, Kendra, ducked her head in acquiescence. "Of course, sir. Would you like a coffee or a latte while you wait?"

"I'm good."

While Kendra made the necessary call, Clint moved toward the wall of fame on the far side of the massive lobby. Dozens of photos of the partners attending various fundraisers and city events adorned the sleek beige wall that served as a canvas. Numerous framed accolades of the firm's accomplishments hung proudly among the photos. Despite his best efforts, bitterness reared its ugly head. Clint rarely allowed that old prick of defeat to needle him anymore. He turned away from the reminders of what he would never have. He was only human; the occasional regression was unavoidable.

He'd done well enough for himself. His law degree had come in handy more than once in his law enforcement career. It gave him an edge in his new venture as a private investigator. If money had been his solitary goal, he would have accepted one of the far more lucrative opportunities he had been offered during his college years.

"Mr. Hayes?"

Clint grinned, then checked the expression as he turned to Kendra. "Yes."

"Mr. Farago will see you now." She gestured to the marble-floored corridor that disappeared into the belly of the enormous building. "Take the elevator to the fourth floor and Darrius, his assistant, will be waiting for you."

With a nod, Clint fastened the top one of the two buttons on his jacket and followed the lady's directions. When he reached the fourth floor the doors slid open with a soft whoosh and revealed a more intimate, but equally luxurious lobby.

Smiling broadly, a young man, twenty-two or -three, met him in the corridor. His slim-fit charcoal-gray suit had the look and style of an Italian label way above his pay grade, suggesting he either came from money or his boss handed out nice bonuses.

"Good morning, Mr. Hayes. My name is Darrius. May I get you a refreshment?"

"No thanks." Clearly Farago's tastes hadn't changed. The assistant, a paralegal most likely, was young, handsome and no doubt hungry. A man did things when he was hungry he might not otherwise do. Clint knew this better than most.

"Very well. This way, sir."

A few steps to the right and Darrius rapped on the first door to the left and then opened it. He gifted Clint with a final smile and disappeared, closing the door behind him.

Farago got to his feet and reached across his desk. "Clint, it's been a while." They exchanged a quick handshake.

"I hear you're scheduled to make partner before the year is out." Clint had nudged a few contacts last night in addition to his internet research. Farago was on his way up at this esteemed firm. Good for him. He'd done his time. Going on eight years now. Still, Clint couldn't help wondering how far his old *friend* had gone this time to ensure his next step up the corporate ladder. He seriously doubted this leopard had changed his spots.

Farago gestured to the chair in front of his desk and settled back into his own. "It's a carrot they dangle when you reach a certain level. Time will tell, I guess."

Clint grunted an acknowledgement.

"So." Farago leaned back in his leather chair. "What brings you to see me after all these years?"

There were many things Clint could have said—payback, for example—but he elected to keep the threats to himself. He had learned that all things come back around in time. Karma truly was a bitch.

As if Farago had read his mind, he fidgeted a bit. Clint could almost swear he saw a sheen of sweat forming on the man's forehead.

"I have a few questions—between old friends— about your colleague, Natalie Drummond."

Farago lifted his head and said, "Ah. I'm certain you're aware, of course, the firm requires we sign confidentiality agreements."

"No doubt." Clint stared straight into his eyes. "I'm equally certain you understand I wouldn't be here if it wasn't essential. So, why don't we cut to the chase? I need information and you *need* to give it to me."

The flush of anger climbed from the collar

of Farago's crisp white shirt and quickly spread across his face. "I see."

"I'm glad we understand each other." Clint had no desire to waste time or energy debating the issue.

Farago's glare was lethal. "What is it you want to ask?"

"You've worked with Natalie for the past four or so years. Until her accident had she suffered any professional issues?"

A haughty chuckle and a roll of the eyes warned that whatever Farago had to say it wouldn't be complimentary. "She had a clerkship with one of our esteemed state court justices before coming on board. Some of us had to do our time performing grunt work here at the firm, but not Natalie. The Drummond name and the recommendation of the justice ensured she started with the cream of the crop cases." Another of those unpleasant smirks. "The rumor was, before her accident she was about to become the youngest partner in the firm." He exhaled a big sigh. "I'll never understand why; she wasn't even that good."

Clint clenched his jaw to the count of three to hold his temper, then asked, "Tell me about the cases she worked in the months leading up to her injury."

Farago made a face. "Let's see. The White case—a mercy killing."

Clint remembered the one. An eighty-year-old husband allowed his dying wife to end her suffering with a bottle of the opiates prescribed by her oncologist. The video they made with the wife's iPhone proved the key piece of evidence that turned the tide with the jury. The woman made her own choice, the only thing the husband did was open the bottle since her arthritic hands couldn't manage the feat.

"Other than that one, there was the Thompson versus Rison Medical Center—a medical malpractice case." Farago turned his palms up. "Those are the primary ones I recall without prowling through databases."

Thompson was the case Clint wanted to hear about. The firm represented the medical center. "Thompson versus Rison Medical Center didn't go down the way anyone expected. Your client was damned lucky."

Farago shrugged. "I don't know. Lots of people claim injuries or trouble with medical facilities or their employees; those claims aren't always based on fact. Emotion can become the center of the case, making it doubly difficult for the defendant's attorneys."

"There's no other case that comes to mind?" Clint pressed.

Farago shook his head. "As I recall, those two pretty much took up her time that year. Why all the questions about Natalie? Is she being investigated?"

Clint ignored his questions. "Her accident was a lucky break for you. You took over her spot on the legal team and the win for Rison Medical Center put *you* on the partners' radar."

Another nonchalant shrug lifted Farago's shoulders. "The win would have put anyone involved on the partners' radar. It was a *huge* lawsuit. We performed above expectations and saved our client a fortune."

"The rumor mill had Thompson pegged as the winner until the bitter end," Clint reminded him. Clint recalled well the day the jury returned with the verdict, he'd been damned surprised. It wouldn't be the first time a sharp legal team had pulled a client's fat out of the fire. Whatever his history with Farago, the man was a good attorney. He just wasn't always a good man.

Clint retrieved a business card that provided his name and cell number. "Call me if you think of anything interesting to pass along on the subject."

Farago studied the card. "You aren't with the BPD anymore?"

Clint smiled. "I decided to come to work with my old boss in her private investigations agency. I'm sure you know Jess Harris Burnett." He stood. "We're taking on the cases no one else can solve." He gestured to the door. "Which office is Natalie's?"

The look on Farago's face was priceless. His eyes bulged. His jaw fell slack. It was almost worth the loss of the career Farago had stolen from Clint a decade ago.

But not quite.

6:50 p.m.

NATALIE WATCHED THE man driving as they moved through the darkening streets. Dusk came a little earlier every day, reminding her that the year was barreling toward an end. It didn't seem possible that she'd lost so much of the past twenty-four months. She didn't want to lose any more. She wanted her life back.

"You don't have to stay with me every minute," she announced to the silence. Neither of them had spoken since leaving the parking garage. She'd worked well beyond the number of hours allowed by her medical release and Clint had insisted on taking her to dinner. "I'm quite capable of taking care of myself, the incident in my kitchen yesterday morning notwithstanding."

Clint smiled. She liked his smile. He was quite attractive for a PI. She'd had her fair share of dealings with private investigators. Most of whom had been older and far less easy on the eyes. In addition to attractive, Clint was well educated and his instincts appeared quite good. He wasn't the only one doing research. She'd done quite a bit herself last night after he left. Clint Hayes possessed a law degree from Samford. He'd graduated with highest honors, but then he'd turned to law enforcement. There was a story there; she just hadn't found it yet. He dressed particularly well. The suit was no off-the-rack light wool ready-for-wear. Neither was the shirt or the shoes. When did private investigators start earning such a high salary?

"Feel free," he glanced at her as he made the turn into the restaurant, "to say whatever is on your mind."

A blush heated her cheeks. She doubted he had any idea of what precisely was on her mind. She might as well see just how good his perceptive powers were. "You went to law school, yet chose a different career path. I wondered what happened to divert your course."

He parked in the crowded lot and shut off the engine. The interior of the car fell into near darkness with nothing more than a distant streetlamp reaching unsuccessfully through the night. When he turned to her it was difficult to read his face, but his voice when he spoke telegraphed a clear message.

"I made the decision I needed to make. I don't

think about it and I don't talk about it. Next question?"

The cool tone was so unexpected that Natalie's heart beat a little faster. "I apologize for making you uncomfortable. I was merely curious."

"I'm very good at what I do, Ms. Drummond. Very good. I'll spend every moment with you and on your case until we find the truth. But—"

Her ability to breathe failed her.

"I am not here to satisfy your curiosity about *me*."

Before she could find her voice, he emerged from the car and walked around to her side. Natalie wasn't sure whether to feel incensed or chastised. When he opened the door she finally remembered to unbuckle her seat belt.

She exited the car. He shut the door and, from all appearances, that would have been the end of it.

"Wait."

He turned back to her and with the soft glow of the restaurant lights she could see his expression well enough to know he wasn't angry...it was something else. Had her question injured him somehow? She blinked and wrestled with the best way to handle the situation. Since her injury she rarely grabbed on to the right emotions much less the proper words in a timely manner. She had taught herself to resist emotion and to react with the cool calm for which she had once been known in the courtroom.

"I apologize for asking such a personal question. I'm afraid the injury has left me with far fewer filters than I once possessed. I hope you'll accept my apology."

He nodded, his only consolation to acceptance. "I had dinner here last week. The salmon is incredible."

"Does your expense account cover this restaurant?" The words were out of her mouth before Natalie could stop them. She squeezed her eyes shut and shook her head.

Clint touched her arm and she opened her eyes. "This one is on me," he assured her, his tone the deep, warm one she had grown to associate with him.

Before she could argue about who would pay, he ushered her through the entrance and she decided to stop trying so hard…at least for the next hour or so.

Southwood Road
9:20 p.m.

AS HE HAD last evening, Clint insisted on going into the house first. Her sister had phoned to say she was coming to spend the night but she would be late. Natalie wanted to tell her not to bother but she wouldn't pretend she wasn't terrified at the idea of being alone at night after the ordeal with the intruder. The idea made little sense since it had been broad daylight when she shot the man in her kitchen.

You did shoot him...didn't you?

The idea that she was second-guessing herself again after finally, finally reaching the place where she felt she'd regained her confidence made her sick to her stomach.

Clint paused at the bottom of the staircase and she raised her hand. "No need to check upstairs. The security system was armed. I'm sure it's fine."

"I wouldn't be able to sleep tonight if I wasn't thorough."

Natalie nodded, surrendering. "I probably wouldn't, either," she confessed.

Side by side they moved up the staircase. She was never able to climb or descend the stairs without admiring the painting of her family as it had once been. Life had felt so safe and so happy then. It seemed unfair she'd lost both her parents before she was thirty. Particularly since they had both been healthy and vibrant. If they were still alive, what would they think of Natalie and her sister? Would her father be proud Heath had been so successful following in his footsteps? Certainly April had become every bit the fund-raising and society queen their mother had been. Natalie sometimes regretted that her sister had not chosen a career path, but in truth what she did was immensely important to the community.

"You grew up in this house?" Clint asked as they reached the landing.

She nodded. "My grandfather built it. He and my grandmother lived here until they died. My parents did, as well. I suppose I will, too." She caught herself before she suggested it was her turn for a personal question. Not a good idea. His assignment necessitated the asking of questions.

"My father died when I was at Samford," he said, somehow understanding her need for reciprocity. "My mother remarried and moved to Arizona a few years ago."

"You miss them? I still miss mine."

He checked the first of the half dozen bedrooms as well as each of the en suite baths. Just when she was certain he didn't intend to answer, he said, "I do. My mother calls a couple of times a month, but she rarely gets home anymore. I should visit her more often but I don't think Oscar likes me."

He chuckled and the sound made Natalie smile. He had a nice laugh for a man who preferred not to talk about his early career decisions.

Silence lapsed between them as they moved through room after room. He took extra care with the upstairs den and the balcony that overlooked the rear gardens. The French doors were locked, the security monitor in place. She and her sister had played here as children. In the gardens, too; but not without the nanny. The Drummond name and money had always been a target.

When they reached Natalie's bedroom, she touched his arm. "Please, ignore what you see in my private space."

His dark eyes held hers for a long beat. "I understand the need for personal privacy, Natalie. You can trust me with your secrets."

As foolish as it sounded, she did. Perhaps her need for his understanding was because his academic background was so similar to hers. If he believed her…then maybe she wasn't losing her mind.

The room was neat and freshly cleaned. Suzanna was a perfectionist and perhaps was afflicted with more than a little OCD. On the table next to Natalie's side of the king-size bed were the first of the many notes to herself. Those on the bedside table reminded her to shut off the alarm and to plug and unplug her cell phone as well as to put it into the pocket of whatever jacket, sweater or coat she would wear for the day.

Each drawer of the room's furnishings was labeled with what would be found stored in that space. In the closet her clothes were arranged in groupings so that whatever she needed for the day was together. No rifling through blouses or shoes and trying to match. April helped her keep her wardrobe arranged. The first time Natalie left the house with a mismatched ensemble, her sister was mortified and insisted on ensuring it never happened again. Natalie supposed it was necessary since her appearance reflected on the firm as well as the family name. April reminded Natalie that she'd had impeccable taste before the fall. Natalie still liked the same things, she simply felt confused at times when she attempted to put together an ensemble.

One of many things she missed about her old self. Thankfully the occurrences of confusion were becoming more rare, or they had been until the intruder. Most likely she would be fine without all the notes to remind her. She simply hadn't found the courage to do away with them yet. *Soon*, she promised herself. Her real hesitation was the fear of failure. As long as the notes were there, she didn't have to face her potential inability to work without them.

Though her walk-in closet was quite generously sized, somehow Clint's broad shoulders and tall, lean frame overwhelmed the intimate space. It was then that his aftershave or cologne teased her senses once more. She had noticed the subtle scent in the car. Something earthy and organically spicy as if it were as natural to his body as his smooth, tanned skin. She was immensely grateful she hadn't lost her sense of smell. Many who suffered TBIs weren't so fortunate.

He turned and she jumped. "Sorry." She took a deep breath and followed him into the en suite. There were more notes here. The ones that told her in what order to do her nightly ritual, those that reminded her of where things were stored. Like the others, she didn't rely on them as much as she had before. This time when he turned to her she felt the weight of his sympathy.

There was nothing since the injury that hurt her more—not the ongoing healing, not the physical therapy, not even the endless hours of analyzing by the shrinks—than the looks of pity in the eyes of anyone who learned the full scope of her loss.

"The house is clear. I'll stay until your sister arrives."

She wanted to argue. Damn it, she really did. She wanted to tell him in no uncertain terms that she was perfectly fine and capable of taking care of herself as she always had been. Except…she wasn't so sure of that anymore. "Thank you."

As they descended the stairs, he said, "Coffee would be good."

With monumental effort she smiled. "I am very good with a coffee machine."

He paused before taking the next step down. "I have a feeling you're very good at many things, Natalie."

Whether he truly meant the words or not, she appreciated the effort. No one had given her a compliment in a very long time.

Chapter Four

11:45 p.m.

Natalie woke with a start, her breath coming in short, frantic bursts as the images from her dreams faded. Sweat dampened her skin. She threw back the blanket and shivered as the cool air swept over her damp body.

She tried to make sense of the vivid, broken images. Pages and pages of briefs or reports rifling past…the words flying from the paper, turning to something gray—like ash or smoke. The empty pages fell into a heap and ignited, the flames growing higher and higher, until she could feel the burn.

Natalie sat up on the edge of the bed. She stared at the clock radio on the bedside table, the time mocking her. She hadn't slept soundly through the night without the aid of medication after the fall. Finally, six months ago she'd managed the feat without the pills. Much to her frustration, the dark whispers that started month before last had taken that accomplishment away from her. As if her subconscious was somehow rutted and the wheels of her mind were destined to slide off into that same rut, she woke at this time every night. A scarce few minutes before the grandfather clock downstairs started the deep, familiar dong of the midnight hour.

Had April come in without waking her? Natalie had intended to stay up to make sure her sister arrived safely, but she'd fallen asleep on her bed still dressed in her work clothes. Surely April was here and Clint had gone home. The idea that he might still be sitting in his car on the street made her cringe. The wood floor was cool beneath her bare feet as she crossed the dark room. If her sister was here and asleep there was no need to wake her. Maybe Natalie would be lucky and this would be one of those nights she was able to get a few more hours of sleep before dawn.

The hall outside her door was as dark as her room. She slipped toward the far end to the room her sister had used as a child. Growing up, Natalie had slept in the one directly across the hall. For reasons she couldn't explain, after the fall she no longer felt safe in that room. The nurse and April had moved her into their parents' room. April insisted it was past time they'd stored their

parents' things anyway. From her bed, Natalie remembered watching her sister oversee the packing. At the time, Natalie had to be reminded over
and over what April was doing. She hadn't been
able to hang on to a thought for more than a few
minutes. Her memory as well as her ability to
function had been in pieces—a part here or there
worked, but none operated together.

Downstairs the chiming of the hour began,
the deep sound echoing all through the silent
house. As Natalie reached her sister's bedroom
the sound of voices stopped her. Natalie held her
breath and listened. The voices were too low—
whispers almost—to understand, but one was
definitely April. The tinkling of her soft laugher
was unmistakable. The other voice was deeper,
definitely male.

Had David decided to stay overnight as well?

Funny, all these weeks she'd been hearing those
whispered voices and not once had she been able
to identify one of them. Natalie turned and made
her way back toward her own room. Though she
and David had never really been friends, he had
visited Natalie at the hospital and then the rehab
facility almost as often as April. Since she'd been
home he had ensured the gardener had everything
he needed. She supposed she should try and think
better of him.

"Not in this lifetime," she muttered. David's

arrogance and distance were two things she distinctly remembered about the past.

The incessant beep of the alarm warned that someone had opened the front door. Natalie's pulse stumbled, then started to race. She had locked the door, hadn't she? Obviously she'd set the alarm. Had April remembered to set it when she arrived? Natalie darted toward her bedroom before she remembered the gun was no longer there. It was missing along with the man she shot. Her cell was downstairs in her purse.

Fear burned through her veins.

Laughter followed by April's voice echoed up from the entry hall. "I'm here. Night. Night. I'll be home in the morning."

The sound of the front door closing and the alarm being reset had Natalie turning to stare toward her sister's bedroom. If her sister was downstairs just coming in…

Natalie's heart sank. Heath was right. She was hallucinating again.

Oxmoor Road
Wednesday, September 21, 9:05 a.m.

DR. SADIE MORROW considered the confession long enough without saying anything to have Natalie ready to scream in frustration. Last night was the first time since the voices began that Natalie could unequivocally confirm that she had been dreaming or hallucinating. She had heard April's voice in her room when April couldn't possibly have been there. Was she having some sort of breakdown? Had her decision to return to work prompted a downward spiral? She had no real cases of her own. There was no true pressure related to her work at this point. How could it be too much stress?

Was her career over? The doctors, including the one assessing her right now, had assured Natalie that she would be able to return to work. She might never be exactly the same as she was before, but she would be able to have a life and a career. Emotion burned in her eyes and she wanted to scream.

"Perhaps," Sadie announced, breaking the tension, "you were sleep walking. What you heard may have been a dream."

This was the assessment Sadie had stood by since the first time Natalie mentioned the voices. "It didn't feel like a dream," Natalie argued.

"The vivid ones rarely do. It's very possible you were asleep and the sound of your sister's voice when she came in woke you."

This was the second day this week that Natalie had shown up at Sadie's office for an emergency consultation. Her friend had other patients. Natalie felt guilty taking up her time like this, but the fear that she was losing her mind overrode all other concerns.

"I was doing fine until I went back to work." The conclusion hung like a millstone around her neck. What was she going to do with her life if she couldn't have her career? What client would want to be represented by an attorney struggling with the after effects of a TBI?

"Natalie, you've been a textbook case in success. Every aspect of your recovery has been the most optimistic of outcomes. This is a bump along the path, that's true. However, I'm confident whatever is triggering these events will pass. I don't think you need to be overly concerned at this point."

Natalie laughed, the sound sad. "You do realize that's my high school BFF talking, don't you?" She shook her head. "I mean, you are the only person who believes there is a medical explanation for the event that happened in my kitchen. I still believe I shot an intruder with my father's gun while the police are convinced I'm a nutcase."

Sadie stood and came around her desk to sit next to Natalie. She took Natalie's hands in hers. "You have to trust me when I say I do not believe you're having a breakdown. Whatever is going on, there is another explanation. New memories may be trying to surface. Your mind may be misinterpreting the memories."

Natalie sighed. "I didn't tell April what happened last night. I just hurried back to my room and pretended to be asleep when she checked on me." The embarrassing emotion she tried so hard to hold back burned like fire in her eyes. She did not want to cry. She needed to be strong. She wanted to move on from this.

"It's not necessary to tell anyone else about this, Natalie. Let's just see how it goes. I'm completely convinced we're dealing with memories. The shooting in your kitchen may be a memory from a case you once worked or studied. What you heard last night could have been a memory from when you and April were teenagers."

Natalie dabbed at her eyes with the back of her hand. "All right. That's the theory I'll operate under for now."

Sadie gave her a hug. "Now, tell me about the man in the lobby. He is incredibly handsome."

"Clint Hayes. He's the PI I hired to figure out what happened to the guy I shot." The memory of the sound of the bullet discharging from the barrel made her flinch. Had the intruder taken her father's weapon? It was the only explanation. She had the weapon in her hand and she fired it. The .38 had been loaded. Her father had kept it that way. As girls she and April had been lectured many times on how that drawer in her father's bedside table was off limits. Their father had explained over and over the reason he kept the weapon next to his bed and their responsibility for staying away from it. He'd put the fear of God in them at an early age. Neither of them had ever touched the drawer much less the weapon for fear of their father's wrath. As it turned out, the weapon had been outfitted with a trigger guard. It wasn't until after her parents' deaths that Natalie had discovered and removed the guard.

"So, he's your bodyguard, too?"

The twinkle in Sadie's blue eyes was teasing. Natalie managed a smile. "I guess he is. He takes his work very seriously." And he was handsome. He was also nice, though he did apparently have a few skeletons of his own.

"I'm glad you hired him." Sadie patted her hand. "Better to be safe than sorry."

Natalie stood. "I should go so you can get back to your scheduled patients. Your secretary is going to start locking the door when she sees me coming."

Sadie dismissed the idea with a wave of her hand. "Nonsense. Now, I expect to hear from you if there are any more unsettling episodes."

"Count on it." Natalie made her way back to the lobby. As if he sensed her coming, Clint set the magazine he held aside and pushed to his feet.

How was it that she suddenly felt safer just knowing he was waiting for her?

CLINT WALKED NATALIE to her car. Like yesterday, she insisted on driving herself about. Reasonable considering she'd only been cleared to drive again four months ago. No one appreciated the everyday personal freedoms until they were lost. Though he had never suffered an injury like the one Natalie struggled to overcome, he was more than a little familiar with the battle to conquer life's stumbling blocks.

She hit the fob to unlock the doors and he opened the driver's side for her. "You're headed to the office?"

"Yes." She hesitated before settling behind the steering wheel. "Will you be coming as well?"

Clint had planned to meet Lori and Harper for coffee to discuss Natalie's case once she was settled in at her office. Maybe he still would, but the distinct note of hope in her question gave him pause. "I have a meeting, but—"

"Really, you don't need to watch me every moment." She arranged her lips into a smile that failed to reach her eyes. "I'm fairly certain no one is going to attack me at my office. Besides, if the police are correct in their conclusions my concerns are wholly rooted in my imagination."

She turned to get into the car and he touched

her arm, stopping her though she didn't face him. "My meeting can wait. Why don't you tell me what happened to bring you here this morning? The appointment wasn't on your calendar."

He'd skimmed her calendar yesterday. Her next scheduled appointment with Dr. Morrow was two weeks away. From the moment she greeted him at her front door this morning he'd recognized something was off.

"Last night I… I think I started hallucinating again." She turned to him and the fear and pain in her expression tugged hard at his protective instincts. "I haven't done that in nearly a year."

"The office can wait. Let's go back to your home. I want you to walk me through exactly what you saw and heard last night."

She squeezed her eyes shut for a moment. "Dr. Morrow said it may have been a dream. But… I can't trust my judgment."

"Your judgment seems fine at work all day and all evening with me. Why is it that all these strange events only occur when you're at home alone?"

Her response was slow in coming. "I don't know. I guess I feel more relaxed at home." She shook her head. "Or because that's where the fall happened. Two psychiatrists as well as Sadie have analyzed me and they all seem to agree on one thing: my brain is trying to recover the pieces and the pieces don't always fall into their proper place leading to misinterpretations. I can't trust... *myself.*"

Clint resisted the urge to take her in his arms and comfort her. Not a smart move. The hair on the back of his neck suddenly stood on end. He glanced at the street, surveyed the block. The distinct feeling they were being watched nudged him. "Let's talk about this in a more private setting."

She nodded and climbed into her car. He closed the door and headed back to his Audi. He'd done some reading on TBI patients and he couldn't argue that Natalie might very well be mistaking dreams for reality or hallucinating, but his gut definitely disagreed with the conclusion.

As he followed her onto the street, Clint considered the reasons someone might want to hurt Natalie. Her parents had been gone for more than three years when the fall down the stairs occurred. It seemed unlikely to him that a sibling would have waited so long to take action if the motive was the family estate. No, his money was on her professional life—specifically the Thompson versus Rison Medical Center case.

Until Natalie was hospitalized, the case was leaning toward a win for Thompson, which would certainly have had the firm under serious pressure to turn it around. Once she was out of the picture, the tide quickly turned. Clint had no proof of his working theory but it was far too large a coincidence to ignore. Though he'd had to walk away from the law career he'd expected to have, he'd maintained a few good contacts. He had never been able to resist keeping up with the David and Goliath cases. Seeing the underdog win made him very happy.

Natalie's car suddenly swerved. Tension snapped through Clint. She barreled off the road into the lot of a supermarket, crashing broadside into a parked car.

His pulse hammering, Clint made the turn and skidded to a stop next to her car. He jumped out and rushed to her. Thank God no one was in the other vehicle. Natalie sat upright behind the steering wheel. The deflated air bag sagged from the steering wheel. The injuries she may have sustained from the air bag deploying ticked off in his brain.

He tried to open the door but it was locked. He banged on the window. "Natalie! Are you all right?"

She turned and stared up at him. Her face was flushed red, abrasions already darkening on her skin. His heart rammed mercilessly against his sternum as she slowly hit the unlock button. He yanked the door open and crouched down to get a closer look at her.

"Are you hurt?" he demanded.

"I'm not sure." She took a deep breath as if she'd only just remembered to breathe. "I don't understand what happened. I was driving along and the air bag suddenly burst from the steering wheel." She reached for the steering wheel and then drew back, uncertain what to do with her hands. "I don't understand," she repeated.

"I'm calling for help." Clint made the call to 9-1-1 and then he called his friend, Lieutenant Chet Harper. Every instinct cautioned Clint that Natalie was wrong about not being able to trust herself.

There was someone else—someone very close to her—that she shouldn't trust. He intended to keep her safe until he identified that threat.

Chapter Five

"Good news, Ms. Drummond."

The ER doctor who looked ridiculously young to be a doctor and seriously disheveled as if he'd worked a twenty-four-hour shift shuffled into the room with Natalie's chart. She was certainly ready for some good news. Her face and chest were sore from the impact of the damned air bag.

How on earth had this happened?

"You're going to be sore and bruised, but no fractures. Your neuro screening was great. You're a lucky lady."

Natalie knew she should feel lucky, yet she didn't. "Thank you, Doctor. Does that mean I can leave now?"

She had spent more than her fair share of time in hospitals and she had no desire to stay in this one another minute. She picked up her jacket and pulled it on, groaning in the process. He wasn't kidding about her being sore. She felt as if she'd had a collision with…another car. Funny thing was, she had. Except the other car hadn't been moving. She'd read briefs on legal cases related to air bags malfunctioning; she just hadn't expected it to happen to her. Wasn't that the way it always turned out?

"As soon as the nurse brings your release papers, you're free to go." The doctor flashed her a weary smile as he headed for the door. "Try to keep it between the lines."

"Thank you. I'll do my best." When he'd gone, she blew out a big breath. How was she supposed to keep her car between the lines if the air bag got in her way? She was no mechanic but she understood the air bag deployment wasn't supposed to happen. Events like this morning's were the sort that resulted in lawsuits.

The car had been a gift to herself just a year before the fall. She'd only started driving again four months ago. The vehicle scarcely had ten thousand miles on it. She should call the manufacturer and see about any recalls.

A soft rap on the door drew her attention there as Clint entered the room. "The doctor tells me you're ready to go."

"Beyond ready," she assured him.

He offered his hand. She felt somehow comforted by the small gesture as she placed her hand in his and climbed down from the examining table. Thankfully the nurse arrived with the necessary documents for her escape. As they exited the ER lobby she dug for her sunglasses, but remembered she had been wearing them when she crashed. They were likely still in her car, possibly broken.

"Do you know which towing company took my car?"

Clint opened the front passenger-side door of his car. "I had it towed to the lab."

Natalie held her hand above her eyes to block the sun so she could see his face better. "What lab?"

"The BPD's forensic lab, for testing. We need to understand what caused the air bag to deploy."

A stone-cold certainty settled in the pit of her stomach. "You think someone tampered with it."

"I do."

"My God." She dropped into the passenger seat for fear she'd fall if she remained standing. Could someone have really done such a thing? She had consoled herself with the idea that the intruder in her home was likely there to steal, but deep inside she feared it was more personal. Was it possible that Clint really believed her?

He was sliding behind the steering wheel before she realized he'd moved. "You really do think someone wants to harm me? That it's not my imagination?"

"Isn't that why you hired me?"

She stared into his dark eyes. She'd been so determined to prove she wasn't losing her mind and that she really had shot someone she hadn't stopped to consider what she truly believed about the intruder.

"I don't know." She pressed a hand over her mouth to hide the way her lips trembled. Of course she knew. She was not naive. Of course this was about hurting her—possibly killing her. Why would anyone want to harm her?

Those dark whispers she had tried so hard to close out just before she drifted off to sleep each night these past eight or so weeks nudged her now, echoing deep in her mind. She closed her eyes and let them come. Laughter, soft, feminine…then the raised voices—a man and a woman. She couldn't understand the words or identify the voices. Was it a real memory? Something from before her fall? Something from childhood?

The blare of a car horn snapped her eyes open. Air filled her lungs in a rush before she realized she'd been holding her breath. Natalie blinked a couple of times to clear the fog. The doctors had explained that pieces of memory from different times often tried to blend, making any memories surfacing more confusing than anything else.

God knew she'd heard plenty of arguments. Clients argued. Colleagues argued. This felt more personal. She and Steven had argued. Maybe the voice was hers. She frowned. It could be a memory of one of their arguments. The laughter could be hers or April's. The sounds reminded her of what she'd heard last night. So maybe the laughter was April from years ago when they'd both lived at home and April had sneaked more than one boyfriend into her bedroom. It was a miracle their parents never caught her. With her sister staying in her old room it was more than possible those old memories had been triggered.

Natalie had never had a boyfriend she liked enough to risk disappointing her father. Then again, perhaps that was why she was alone right now. She pushed away the idea. Feeling sorry for herself wasn't going to solve this mystery and it certainly wouldn't help her recovery.

As Clint made the turn onto Southwood Road, Natalie said, "I should call for a rental car." She had no idea how long her car would be at the lab and then there would be the repairs. Maybe she should just buy a new one. She shuddered at the idea that someone may have tampered with her car.

"You won't need one for a while."

She waited until he'd parked in front of her home to say, "I don't intend to stay holed up in this house. I can't…do that." As big as her home was, the walls had begun to close in on her well before she had been able to return to work. As long as she had half a brain and the ability to walk she was not staying in the house 24/7 ever again.

When she reached for the door, he put his hand on her arm. "Wherever you go, I go, so I might as well drive."

She wanted to argue but some self-preservation instinct prevented her from doing so.

"This is only temporary, Natalie. We'll get to the bottom of the problem and then you'll have your life back."

The roar of an engine and the squealing of tires had them both turning to see who had charged into the driveway.

April.

"I should have called her." Natalie's sister had a way of hearing the news before it was broadcast anywhere.

April emerged from her Mercedes in a huff and stormed across the cobblestone. "What happened? Why didn't you call me?"

"I'm fine, April. Really."

April glared at Clint. "You don't have my number, Mr. Hayes?"

While Clint poured on the charm and added

April to his contacts list, Natalie watched her sister. She pretended to be angry that no one had called her, but she was actually terrified. April's slim body trembled and she hugged herself. Natalie bit back the emotions threatening. Her sister was so opposite from her. She'd bleached her dark hair blond when they were teenagers and she'd kept it that way. April had claimed it looked better with her blue eyes. They had the same blue eyes. Before she'd bleached her hair people had often asked if they were twins. Except Natalie had always been the frumpier one. A little heavier and a lot more conservative when it came to fashion. April had always needed to set herself apart.

"Why don't we go inside?" Clint asked when April continued her tirade despite his efforts to calm her.

"Just tell me what it is you're doing to help my sister," April demanded.

"April," Natalie warned.

"As soon as we have the forensic report back on the car we'll know more."

April stared at him in disbelief. "Forensic? What does that mean?"

Natalie reached for her sister but she held up a hand. "No," April insisted, "I want to know what he's talking about."

"I believe," Clint said, drawing her attention back to him, "someone tampered with the air bag."

April swung her stunned glare to Natalie. "Is he serious?"

"Yes." There was no point trying to keep the truth from her sister. "Our current working theory is that the intruder and the accident are connected."

"There was no intruder!" April planted her hands on her hips. "You're only hurting yourself going down this path, Natalie." Her sister shook her head. "I'm calling David. He'll know what to do."

Natalie felt taken aback. "Is that a threat of some sort?" It felt exactly like a threat.

April appeared startled. "Of course it isn't a threat. I'm... I'm just worried about you and I don't trust him." She arrowed a contemptuous look at Clint. "I know about you, Mr. Hayes. My sister may not be herself just now, but she's no fool. She'll see through you soon enough."

With that profound statement April strode away.

Natalie turned to Clint. "What's she talking about?"

"We should go inside."

Numb, Natalie followed him.

If her life felt upside down before, it was totally ripped apart now.

CLINT SAT ON the sofa and waited for Natalie to begin her interrogation. She'd insisted on making tea after he'd done his walk-through of the house. The proverbial wait for the water to boil had felt like forever. Eleven years. He'd put this business behind him more than a decade ago. He'd made up his mind he didn't care and he'd walked away. He'd applied to the police academy and moved on. All those years as a detective had driven home the point that stuff happened and sometimes good people got the short end of the stick.

Natalie returned her cup to its dainty little saucer. The delicate china with its pink rose pattern reminded him of her vulnerability. The cup would shatter if dropped despite its ability to withstand being fired at thousands of degrees. Natalie Drummond might be tough as nails but she had her breaking point and someone was pushing her further and further in that direction.

"What did April mean when she said she knew about you?"

There were some secrets a man couldn't keep forever no matter how hard he tried. No matter how badly he didn't want to look back. The only surprising part was that April had discovered his secret. There were only a handful of people who knew that part of his history. Farago, the bastard, had likely put in a call to the sister. One of these days he was going to get his. Clint hoped he was around to watch.

"It has something to do with why you chose not to pursue a career as an attorney," Natalie suggested.

She'd asked him about that before and he'd done what he always did, he'd brushed her off. Making that leap now was the reasonable route to take. "It does."

"Is it relevant to my case?"

"No." Was she offering a way out of this discussion?

She nodded. "I see. Well." Shoulders squared, she picked up her cup. "I don't see any reason to discuss the matter."

He wanted to be relieved but he understood this would not be the last time the issue came back to haunt him. "Why put off the inevitable? April feels the issue is relevant to my trustworthiness."

Natalie lifted her chin. "But I don't. Despite recent events, my sister is not my keeper."

The seed of doubt had been planted. Clint was well aware how this worked. The subject might feel irrelevant at the moment but in the middle of the night when she couldn't sleep it would nag at her.

"My father worked in a factory," he began. "My mother operated a daycare in our house for the neighborhood children. Together they made enough to keep a roof over our heads and to fall above the income level for any sort of government aid. There was no money for college, much less law school." He resisted the urge to stand and pace. "I was a smart kid. I didn't get the kind of scholarships the athletes received, but it was enough to get me in the door. The rest, however, was up to me."

"So you worked your way through school," Natalie offered. "There's no shame in hard work. College is expensive. Law school is even more costly."

She couldn't hide the automatic guilt she clearly felt for growing up rich when she heard stories like his. No matter, when she heard the rest that guilt would shift into outrage and disgust. What the hell?

"I worked as an *escort*." He figured she would comprehend the full implications of the statement without him going into graphic detail.

She sipped her tea, cleared her throat and took a breath. "Do you mean—?"

"I mean exactly what you think I mean. The Alabama State Bar used its morals clause to preclude my admission to the bar based on my character and that was that."

"You did this for…?"

If she blinked too hard the frozen expression on her face would no doubt shatter. Clint almost laughed. He was a damned good investigator. Whether he'd delivered pizza or pleasure during college should be of no consequence to the job he had to do now. "Five years."

The duration of his early career startled her and the dainty cup almost slipped from her slim fingers. "I see."

No. She didn't see at all. There were other things he could tell her, like the fact that he earned more in his first year than the average attorney did in his first four. He'd had a high-end operation, not a street corner. His clients had been the rich and famous of Alabama. By the time he hit law school he had invested widely and wisely. He could retire now, if he chose, on the investments he'd made. None of that would matter. He saw the horror and disbelief in her eyes.

He stood, fury and frustration beating in his pulse, and buttoned his jacket. "You have my number. Let me know if you still require my services. If not, I'll ask the boss to send someone else."

"Sit down, Clint."

Whatever hesitation she'd felt before, there was none in her blue eyes now. He, on the other hand, hesitated. He wasn't apologizing for his past.

"Please," she added.

He ripped the jacket button loose once more and sat. His boss, he still had to work at reminding himself not to call Jess chief, would be the first one to say he didn't care for taking orders. He preferred giving them. That said, he wanted this new venture to work out for all concerned—including the lady staring at him right now. Whether she realized it or not, she needed him.

"I don't care what you did to survive in college. We all did things we might not have done at any other time in our lives." She smiled. "Kudos to you. Law school was tough as hell and still you made it. The State Bar's decision was unfair and antiquated in my opinion. If you ever decide to fight that decision, I would be more than happy to represent you."

Clint did laugh then. "I appreciate the offer, but I'm completely satisfied with my current career."

She drew in a deep breath and immediately pressed a hand to her chest. He imagined she'd be damned sore for a few days. Did she understand she could have been killed in that crash? She could have killed someone else?

"What do we do now? You said my car is at the lab."

"Ricky Vernon, one of the forensic guys at the lab, is sort of a computer geek. He's the best. He'll be able to tell us why the air bag launched prematurely. If the perp left prints or any other evidence, he'll find that, too. If we find evidence a crime was committed, Lieutenant Harper—he leads the BPD's major crimes unit—will give us the full support of his team."

"How long will the lab take?"

"Harper put a rush on the analysis. Vernon will probably work all night if necessary." Clint had seen the guy pull an all-nighter more than once. Damn he missed the team, but working with Jess was where he wanted to be.

A knock on the open door drew Clint's attention there. Suzanna, the housekeeper, stood in the open doorway, her bag draped over her shoulder. "Ms. Natalie, Leonard and I are done for the day unless you need anything else."

Natalie smiled, clearly fond of the older lady. "We're fine, thank you."

"I left chicken salad in the fridge." She turned to Clint. "You take good care of her."

He smiled. Suzanna and her husband had worked for the Drummond family for three decades. "You can count on it, ma'am."

When the housekeeper was gone, Natalie stood. "We should eat."

Clint pushed to his feet. "You go ahead. I'd like to have a look at the garage."

Someone who had access to her home was screwing with Natalie's life. No matter how long the housekeeper and her gardener husband had worked for the family, everyone was a suspect. Even Natalie's sister.

Especially her sister.

Chapter Six

Athens-Flatts Building, 2nd Avenue
7:30 p.m.

The elevator door opened and Natalie's jaw dropped. "Wow. What a view."

Before Clint even invited her to step out of the elevator that opened into the foyer of his condo, she was already walking toward the incredible wall of glass that looked out over downtown Birmingham.

She turned to the man watching her so closely as if he feared her disapproval. "This is the penthouse." She shook her head. "I've always wondered who lived here." She laughed. "Just wow." The view was absolutely amazing.

"It came up for sale last year. The couple who owned it were getting divorced and neither wanted the other to end up with the best party spot in the city."

Natalie lifted her gaze to his. "You bought it for having parties?" She'd spent the past four hours struggling not to think about him having sex with all those women...

Don't think about him that way.

"I've been to my share of parties, but I rarely play the role of host."

She turned back to the view, certain she didn't want him to see the trouble she was having keeping his past occupation out of her head. Had she ever known a man who provided personal services?

No. No, she had not.

"Well, it's a lovely home." There. A perfectly benign statement of the truth.

"I can't take credit for the decorating. I bought the place, furniture and artwork included."

"The previous owners had good taste." She tugged at the collar of her blouse, feeling warm. She'd changed into casual slacks and a blouse and still she felt constricted and...*hot*. "Is it all right if I see the rest of the place?" She had to do something besides stand here and make small talk.

"Of course. I'll grab a few things."

They came to his home so he could pack the clothes and other essentials he would need to stay with her for a few days. The idea of having him right down the hall had abruptly taken on a whole new connotation considering his confession. She refused to linger on the subject. She needed help finding the truth. Clint was helping. End of story.

Natalie waited until he'd disappeared into the master suite, and then she moved in the opposite direction. The main living space was one massive room with that breathtaking view. Lots of gleaming hardwood, sleek granite and stainless steel. The furnishings were a tasteful blend of leather, wood and upholstered pieces. The ceiling soared high overhead where metal pipes and ductwork lent an urban feel. The few art pieces on the muted gray walls were stark and yet somehow compelling. The one that drew her in was the artist's rendering of a city street disappearing into the night. She thought of the way so many pieces of her life had slipped into the darkness. How many more pieces were missing?

Dismissing the worry, she wandered into a short hall that led to a well-appointed bedroom with an en suite. What she decided was the guest room had a similarly spectacular view. The glimpse of her reflection she caught in the mirror over the bathroom vanity made her groan. No black eyes, but her left cheek was bruised. Her chin was scraped. Her chest felt as if the bare skin had been slapped over and over. Was it possible someone close to her had caused the accident? Clint had suggested as much.

"Not possible."

Natalie turned away from the mirror and wandered back into the main living area. She perused the kitchen with its restaurant-quality style. Checked out his wine selection and then rifled through the magazines on the coffee table. She noted the coat closet and the powder room near the elevator.

She roamed back to the sofa. "What now?" she muttered to herself.

"You doing okay out there?"

His deep voice drifted through the space making it seem somehow smaller.

She cleared her throat. "Yes." Natalie rolled her eyes. Evidently the proper etiquette for visiting a friend's home was another of those missing pieces.

"I'm almost finished."

Before she could come up with a good enough reason not to, she strolled in the direction of his voice. A short walk down the hall off the kitchen side of the condo led into the master suite. A jacket landed on the king-size bed. Again there was that stunning view. The city was the first thing he would see when he woke in the morning. She pictured him lying in that enormous bed and—

He appeared from the door to her right, a couple of shirts in hand. "I'll get these in the bag and I'm ready."

She peeked beyond the door to the walk-in

closet. The only place she'd ever seen that many suits was at a men's clothing store. Her father had owned his share of suits, but not even her pompous brother-in-law owned so many. She wandered into the closet, allowed her fingers to drift over the fabrics as she walked past. The suits were arranged according to color and fabric, she realized. Dozens of pairs of shoes. She raised her hand as she reached the starched shirts, her fingers slipping over the smooth fabric. Most were white. There were a few others in pastels and a couple of gray ones. And, sweet Jesus, the silk ties. All hanging neatly behind glass doors.

When she turned around he waited in the doorway, one shoulder braced against the doorframe. "Clothes are an addiction of mine."

Her mouth felt dry. She moistened her lips and managed a smile. "I see that."

He watched her as she turned all the way around for one last look. The idea that he was watching her made her heart beat faster.

"I don't see any jeans or plain old get-my-hands-dirty shirts."

"I have a few."

She laughed, couldn't help herself. "Somehow I can't see you getting your hands dirty under the hood of a car or in the yard."

"You'd be surprised at all the ways I've had my hands dirty."

There was a warning in his words. She heard it clearly and still she dared to move closer. After all, he stood in the doorway. If she intended to escape she had to move past him. "Would I?"

He studied her for another long moment, and then he straightened away from the door. "We should go."

She watched as he grabbed the garment bag and the duffle from the bed. "You have a truly beautiful home." Had she said that already?

He nodded and walked away. She followed. He didn't speak again. Perhaps it was best he didn't. Natalie admired the view one last time before the elevator doors closed.

She squeezed her eyes shut and examined the feelings swirling inside her. There was another piece she'd lost. It startled her a little to suddenly remember it now.

How long had it been since she'd actually been attracted to a man?

Why in the world did her libido have to show up now?

Southwood Road
11:45 p.m.

WHISPERS ROUSED NATALIE. The sound seemed to slide over her skin. Her heart beat faster; her skin tingled. Pages and pages of briefs drifted downward, the words sifting from the paper and falling into a pile. The pages faded into darkness. She was walking...walking toward the light, her fingers sweeping along the soft fabric of suits, rows and rows of suits.

Her eyes opened, she blinked and stared into the darkness for a moment before rolling onto her side. *11:45 p.m.* She came a little more awake, her mind grappling for some sense of the dream.

It was the same every time.

Except this time there had been the suits. It didn't take a degree in psychology to know the suits were about her visit to Clint's home this evening. She pulled the sheet closer and thought about the man who somehow managed to invade her dreams when no one—not even her ex-boyfriend—had done so.

April was furious that Natalie had asked Clint to stay here with her. Her sister wouldn't be back, she'd warned, as long as he was here. David was coming to speak with her tomorrow. Natalie sighed. She had lost all control over her life. On some level she understood her sister's concerns. The brain injury had made a mess of Natalie's ability to function and think for herself—that was true. But the worst was behind her and she continued to get better...the intruder episode aside. She refused to consider last night's hallucinations. Sadie was probably right. Natalie had been dreaming. Dreaming and sleepwalking.

Tinkling laughter floated through the air.

Natalie stilled. Had April changed her mind? She threw back the covers and sat up, dropping her feet to the cool floor. Her sister had sounded quite adamant when she'd called about nine thirty. Maybe guilt had gotten the better of her.

Running her fingers through her hair, Natalie moved soundlessly toward the door. When she reached the hall, she listened. Those soft whispers reached out to her. The sound was definitely coming from her sister's room. She continued toward the sound. The laugh was April's. There was that deeper voice again. Natalie frowned. David hadn't ever spent the night to the best of Natalie's recollection.

Natalie stopped and took a moment to confirm that she was indeed awake.

If she was awake, that meant her sister was in this house, in her old room. Natalie walked to the door of April's childhood room and reached for the knob. She curled her fingers around it, the whispers wrapping around her like a swarm of bees, and turned the knob. She pushed the door inward and reached for the light, the sound of the whispers growing louder and louder.

The bright light made her squint. April's bed was made...the room was empty. The voices vanished.

Natalie closed her eyes and fought the urge to cry. Why did this keep happening?

She turned off the light and closed the door. Maybe she couldn't stop the voices, but she could prevent the incidents from shaking her up so badly. Whatever the voices meant, since they clearly weren't a dream as Sadie had suggested, there was something she needed to remember. Her mind was struggling to bring something to the surface. Fine. She could live with that. Maybe.

She stood in the hall trying to decide what to do next. She could go back to bed and toss and turn for the next couple of hours or she could admit defeat and go downstairs for a glass of wine. Since coming home from the rehabilitation center she had avoided all alcohol. She'd wanted to keep a clear head. Tonight she needed something and she despised the idea of taking the medication again. To reach for the sleeping pills felt like going backward.

She descended the stairs slowly, taking special care to be quiet. Clint had insisted on sleeping on the sofa. He'd put his things in one of the spare bedrooms but he maintained that it was better if he was downstairs. Natalie wasn't sure if that was because downstairs was the most likely entry point for an intruder or if he was trying to protect her reputation.

She felt reasonably certain the part of her reputation that mattered to her, her professional one, was forever damaged already by the TBI. She genuinely appreciated the firm allowing her to return to work, but it was painfully obvious they had no intention of assigning her a case anytime soon.

The lamp on the hall table provided a warm glow in the darkness. The lamp had been turned on each night for as long as she could remember. Neither she nor her siblings had been afraid of the dark, but her mother had insisted there be enough light to get safely down the stairs even in the middle of the night.

As difficult as it was not to peek in at her protector, she managed. He wouldn't appreciate his privacy being invaded. She turned on a light in the kitchen and headed to the wine fridge. She selected a bottle of her favorite white wine, something light and sweet with a slight fizz. A few moments were required to open the bottle. When she'd managed to release the cork, she found a glass and poured a healthy serving.

As she sipped the sweet drink, she stored the bottle in the fridge. She wouldn't risk a second glass. Out of habit she checked the back door before turning out the light and padding back to the staircase. She paused at the bottom, tempted again to peek into the great room.

Instead, she reached for the bannister and

started up the stairs. If she was lucky the wine would help her get back to sleep.

"Having trouble sleeping?"

The sound of his deep voice trapped her breath behind her breastbone. Good thing she had a tight hold on the wine glass. Smile pinned in place, she turned to face him. "I thought I'd try something new." She held up the glass of wine.

"Understandable."

It wasn't until that moment that she allowed her gaze to take in the whole of him. Her attention drifted down from his face to his bare chest. Smooth skin, ripped muscles. His trousers hung low on his hips. For the first time since the fall she tried to remember how long it had been since she'd been kissed by a man—not the I'm-so-sorry pecks from her family. A passionate kiss…the real thing. She couldn't remember. She had no idea when she'd been held, much less kissed. Years. At least two years.

She should never have asked him what April had alluded to about his past. She hadn't needed to know… She hadn't thought about sex in so long. How was it she couldn't banish it from her mind now?

"Good night," he said, interrupting her silent discourse.

She managed a nod. "Good night."

Somehow she turned her back and resumed

her climb up the staircase. Her chest ached but it was from the air bag and not from the loneliness. A frown furrowed her forehead. When had she become so obsessed with being alone?

For the first time she wondered if she would ever have a sex life again. She'd wondered plenty of times if her life would ever be normal but she hadn't afforded any time on the subject of sex. Sadly, it took only one handsome man under the same roof with her to remind her of all that she was missing. Most women her age were married and had a child already.

Before she climbed back into bed she downed the remainder of the wine. Curling up beneath the covers, she sighed and closed her eyes. She sifted through the day's events. She replayed the moments in the car before the air bag hit her in the face and then the hours at the ER. The unpleasant scene in the driveway with her sister and the examination of the garage for signs of foul play. But the last thought tugging at her before she slipped into the darkness was of the man downstairs and how grateful she was to have him here.

She didn't want to be alone.

Chapter Seven

Ricky Vernon passed the report he held to Clint. "Whoever did this knew what he was doing. This was no amateur job. The new sensor was set to engage the air bag as soon as she reached a speed of sixty miles per hour."

Clint glanced at Natalie's BMW. The vehicle would have to be towed to the dealer for repair. All sensors would need to be checked. They couldn't be sure of the true extent of the damage to the electronic systems.

Vernon brushed his brown hair back from his face and adjusted his glasses. His button-down shirt was wrinkled with the sleeves rolled up to his elbows. The trousers bore the same telltale signs of a long day in the lab that had extended through the night and into the next day. Some women considered the rumpled geeky look sexy. Clint wondered if Natalie would prefer Vernon's type.

She'd seemed nervous last night when he interrupted her return to her room with a glass of wine. Had she forgotten he was in the house? Or had she wandered down the stairs wearing a nightgown and no robe on purpose? One narrow strap of the gown had fallen off her shoulder, but the way the hem hit midthigh was the most surprising. She spent her days in those fashionably conservative suits that hardly showed her great body. Last night she'd looked young and innocent, vulnerable. Not the kind of woman who would want a man like him.

Vernon spoke again, drawing Clint's wayward attention. "I'm sorry, what did you say?"

"This isn't the first time this vehicle has been tampered with," the forensic expert repeated. "The main brake line has been repaired. It appears to have been damaged at one time, but the damage was a straight cut, which I find indicative of tampering versus some sort of normal wear and tear. At some point later it was repaired."

"Would this have been recent?" A new kind of tension rippled through Clint.

Vernon shook his head. "Since the vehicle has been garaged for the better part of two years, it would be difficult to guess based solely on the road film and breakdown from routine exposure to the elements. But according to the maintenance log in the glove box, the brakes were repaired twenty-six months ago."

Two months before her fall down the stairs.

"Thanks, Vernon. I owe you one."

"Anytime. Lieutenant Harper said someone's life depended on the findings." Vernon glanced beyond the glass wall that divided the lab from his office on the other side where Natalie waited. Harper and Cook had arrived and were talking to her. "It's nice for a change to be able to help someone before the worst happens."

Far too often by the time evidence like this made it to the lab someone was dead.

Clint was very glad Natalie was unharmed for the most part. He intended to do whatever necessary to see that she stayed that way.

Clint assured Vernon he would get the BMW out of his way as quickly as possible before heading into the office to join Natalie and the detectives. He wasn't looking forward to explaining the details to her. It was difficult enough when a person could accurately assess the threat around them, but for Natalie, there was no way to be certain. There were too many holes in her memory and too many questions she couldn't answer. She had no idea who would want to harm her or for what reason. There was no way at this point to get a fix on the threat.

Harper and Detective Chad Cook had already introduced themselves to Natalie by the time Clint left Vernon to his next task. Harper and Cook were the only two remaining original members of the department's Major Crimes Special Problems Unit. Harper was in command for now. He'd made lieutenant last year. Clint respected both men, called them friends. For him, that was high praise. Clint didn't play well with others.

Harper gave Clint a nod. "Vernon says we got foul play here."

Clint glanced at Natalie who looked even more worried than when they had arrived. "No question."

"I confirmed that the mechanic who repaired the brake line is still employed at the Irondale dealership," Cook explained. "His name's Beckett. His rap sheet is clean other than a DUI back in high school. Harper and I are heading there now to interview him."

Natalie's worry turned to confusion. "I don't understand. What's going on with the brakes?"

"I'll explain the full report to you," Clint promised. To Harper he said, "I'd like to talk to the mechanic first. I don't think we should tip our hand just yet as to police involvement. I'd prefer for whoever is behind this to feel safe for now."

Harper didn't look convinced. "I can give you twenty-four hours, but we can't risk this guy posing a threat to anyone else. You know as well as I do that if he'd do it for a dollar once he'll do it for a dollar again."

Clint couldn't argue his reasoning. "Twenty-four hours is all I need."

"How is this possible?" Natalie turned to Clint. "I haven't taken my car in for service recently. How could he have gained access to it? The only people…"

Her voice drifted off as realization struck her hard. There were very few people with access to her home and unfortunately she was extremely close to those few.

Clint could think of at least four people who were close enough, but which one was motivated enough to commit murder?

IT WAS TOO MUCH.

Natalie couldn't reconcile what the lab's analysis meant. The only people who had access to the house were Suzanna and Leonard, and April, of course. David had a key but he rarely came to the house unless Leonard called him.

Except, how could she be certain?

Before her fall she had worked long hours at the firm. Afterward she'd been in the hospital and then in rehab for months. In the past two months she had spent several hours a day at the office. How could she say for sure who had come and gone? Had Suzanna or Leonard given a key to anyone else? The pest-control service? A plumber or electrician? What about the painters? The house had been given a fresh coat throughout while she was in rehab. The rugs had been cleaned and the floors polished. April had thought it would make Natalie feel better to come home to a fresh start.

Any one of those people coming in and out of the house may have picked up a key.

Or perhaps it was easier to believe a stranger was the culprit rather than someone close to her.

"Harper will check the security cameras at the parking garage next to your office."

Clint's voice startled her back to the present. "I appreciate the department's efforts."

What was the likelihood that someone had come into the garage where she parked while at work and tampered with her car?

None of this made sense.

"You're in a difficult position."

His voice was gentler this time, as if he understood her inability to comprehend the magnitude of what was happening.

"The worst part is I don't know why." She blinked back the tears that burned her eyes. When had she become so emotional? How could she forget? The brain injury had changed some aspects of her personality that might or might not return to normal at some point. "How can I not remember someone who wants to hurt me?"

"Sometimes we remember what we feel comfortable remembering."

The man had done his research. Sadie and the other doctors had said the same thing. The pieces she felt more comfortable with would fall into place first. If she'd had a confrontation or received a threat of some kind, those details might not return until her mind felt ready to accept the burden.

As long as she didn't get murdered first, no problem.

The Irondale dealership wasn't crowded the way it had been three years ago when she'd bought her new BMW. A salesman trailed a couple strolling the lot. Inside, sparsely furnished cubicles where salespersons were either making phone calls or finalizing deals with customers lined one wall. The large customer-service desk stood against the opposite wall while the center of the showroom was occupied by the current models of the carmaker's most popular series. After the formal introductions, the manager, Adam Wheeler, was only too happy to see Natalie and Clint in his private office.

"You must be ready for an upgrade, Ms. Drummond." He smiled broadly as they took their seats. "Mr. Drummond was here just a few days ago to order a new car for his lovely wife."

Her brother hadn't mentioned a new car to Natalie. She wasn't surprised at the omission and it certainly didn't trigger any alarms in her opinion. Like their father, Heath was focused on the business. Other than Thanksgiving and Christmas, the man was generally unavailable.

"Maybe another time," Natalie assured him. "We're actually here about one of your employees. My friend, Mr. Hayes, has a few questions he'd like to ask."

"Of course. I am always happy to brag about my employees. We take great pride in the service we provide." He turned his attention to Clint. "How may I help you, Mr. Hayes?"

"Your mechanic, Mike Beckett, what can you tell us about him?"

"He's a very reliable employee. He has been for the past four years. Always on time and rarely missed a day. We haven't had the first complaint about his work."

"Is he here today?" Clint asked.

"He called in on Monday. Said he needed to get to Denver. Something about his mother being ill."

"Did he indicate when he would return?"

"He did not. His absence left a big hole in our

service schedule. We've been rescheduling appointments all week."

Clint stood. "Thank you, Mr. Wheeler."

Natalie promised to call Wheeler soon about a new car. Considering the damage to her current vehicle, he might be hearing from her sooner than either of them anticipated. She waited until they were back in Clint's car to ask, "What now?"

"Now we talk to your housekeeper and gardener."

"I don't think it's necessary to question Suzanna and Leonard." The idea was ludicrous. She wanted no part of offending them with pointless questions.

"I'm not accusing them of wrongdoing, Natalie," Clint glanced at her as he spoke. "I'm suggesting they may have seen something or someone without realizing it mattered enough to mention. You need to trust me, I know how to handle the situation without stepping on toes or injuring feelings unnecessarily."

He was right. She had no reason to doubt him. "Fine. Just be extra nice, okay?"

The smile he flashed in her direction interrupted the rhythm of her heart in a good way. She thought about the way he'd looked last night only half dressed and standing in that doorway. Her throat went dry. Why was it her sexuality had to reawaken at the worst possible time?

What difference did it make? She had enough trouble at the moment without getting involved romantically with anyone, much less the man who needed to remain focused on finding the source of whatever the hell was going on in her life. Just now, neither he nor she could afford to be distracted.

Natalie leaned back in the seat and closed her eyes. Now was not a good time for getting involved. She cringed at the ludicrous thought and reminded herself that it was difficult to get involved without someone to get involved with. Clint Hayes was the investigator she had hired not her friend or her potential boyfriend.

He was a professional providing a service…

Her fingers tightened on the armrest when she thought of the service he had provided other women during his college days. She wondered what his girlfriend—assuming he had one and she couldn't imagine he didn't—thought of his colorful work history.

Clint received a call on his cell. Natalie tried to gather the gist of the call based on his side of the conversation. He repeated an address that wasn't familiar to her. He thanked the caller then dropped his phone back into his jacket pocket.

She found herself holding her breath as she waited for him to tell her what the call was about. It might have nothing to do with her case.

"That was Harper. Beckett's girlfriend found him at his residence. From the looks of things he had been packing to leave town, but he never made it."

Her heart sank. "He's dead?"

"He is. Has been for at least a day. One gunshot to the chest."

Natalie stopped the rush of thoughts whirling in her head and forced herself to focus. "Is there any way to determine if he tampered with my car or if his murder has anything to do with...me?"

"Harper and Cook are two of the best detectives in the department. If anyone can determine what Beckett was up to the final days and hours of his life, they can."

"I don't understand." Why was this happening? She'd gone to bed one night with nothing more to worry about than the case she was assigned and when she woke up her world had changed. She didn't remember getting up or falling down the stairs. Her first memory was waking up in the hospital with April asleep in the chair next to her bed. At that point Natalie had been in a coma for ten days. "What does this mean?"

"I don't know," Clint admitted as he made the turn onto her street. "But I will find out."

"The whole situation is simply insane." Natalie shook her head, stunned, horrified and frustrated. She didn't realize she'd braced her hand against the console until he wrapped his fingers around hers. He didn't say a word, simply gave her hand a quick, gentle squeeze and then let go. Somehow that basic touch calmed her, made her dare to hope.

Natalie kept her chin up the rest of the drive. Clint pulled into the driveway to find Suzanna and Leonard packing up their SUV. At first Natalie thought perhaps they were merely leaving a little early today, but the back of the SUV was loaded with boxes.

"What on earth?" Natalie climbed out of the car.

Leonard closed the tailgate and moved around to the driver's door without uttering as much as a hello.

"Suzanna, what's going on?"

The older woman faced Natalie, her expression cluttered with dread. "We can't do this anymore, Natalie. It's past time we retired anyway. I left you a letter explaining our feelings."

Natalie shook her head. "I don't understand. You can't do what? Has something happened you haven't told me about?"

"Suzanna!"

The older woman glanced at the SUV. "He doesn't want me to get tangled up in this mess."

"Tangled up in what mess?" They couldn't possibly know about her air bag fiasco or the murder of the mechanic who may have tampered with it. "What in the world are you talking about?"

Suzanna glanced toward her husband once more, but then leaned forward and whispered for Natalie's ears only, "I found the bloody clothes and the gun hidden in your room, Miss Natalie. I don't know what it means, but I can't protect you anymore."

"Suzanna, wait!"

Natalie's words fell on deaf ears. The couple who had taken care of her family's home for three decades loaded up and drove away while she stood helplessly watching.

"What was that all about?"

Natalie looked up at Clint, possibly the last person on the planet who believed in her. "I have no idea."

The mechanic, Beckett, had been shot… Suzanna had found bloody clothes and a gun in Natalie's room.

Could she…no, no, she could never have gone to his home and killed him…but she had shot someone.

Was Mike Beckett the intruder she shot in her kitchen? Why would she have changed clothes and hidden them and the gun before the police came? How could she have moved the body? She hadn't even known his name, much less where he lived. Dear God, had she killed a man?

Chapter Eight

8:59 p.m.

Natalie closed her bedroom door and sagged against it. From the moment Suzanna whispered those horrifying words to her, Natalie had been trying to think of a way to go to bed early without Clint asking questions.

He had almost managed to distract her from her thoughts by making dinner. Like any good hostess, she had tried to help but her fingers had fumbled at every turn. Finally, he'd told her to sit and keep him company. She'd tried to pay attention to the conversation but her mind had whirled with memories and those dark whispers…and fear. Had the man she shot been Mike Beckett? The threat of tears forced her eyes to squeeze shut. The sound of the gun discharging made her jump.

She straightened away from the door and took a

deep breath. Suzanna said the gun and the clothes were hidden in Natalie's room. Shoring up her courage with another deep breath, she began the slow, methodical search of her room, the bathroom and then the closet.

Nothing looked as if it had been moved. What had Suzanna been doing prowling around in here anyway? And wouldn't bloody clothes smell?

Natalie pushed her hanging clothes aside and checked behind them. She searched every shelf and drawer. Then she turned to the white wicker laundry hamper. She removed the lid and at first thought it was empty, but when she leaned down for a closer inspection she realized there was a white garbage bag at the bottom. Hand shaking, she closed her fingers in the plastic and pulled it from the hamper.

Heavy...too heavy to be only clothes.

Her heart started to pound and she sank to the floor.

She opened the bag and the smell of blood made her gag. Covering her mouth and nose with her hand she peered at the contents. A pastel blue suit Natalie didn't readily recognize as her own was wadded up inside. Blood splatter dotted the fabric. Crushed against the suit was a handgun... a .38 exactly like the one her father had kept in his bedside drawer. Just like the one Natalie had used on the intruder.

Natalie scrambled up, stuffed the bag back into the hamper, and ran to the bathroom just in time to lose the wonderful dinner she had forced herself to eat. She washed her face and stared at her reflection in the mirror. Why would she change clothes and hide them and the gun?

Did the bloody clothes have something to do with what Suzanna meant when she said she couldn't protect Natalie any longer?

Protect her from what? Or whom?

Herself?

She should call Clint up here right now and show him what she'd found. He would call his friend Lieutenant Harper…

Natalie bit her trembling lips together. Why couldn't she remember? Had she blacked out between the shooting and the time she actually called for help?

Right now she needed to think and to calm herself. First she had to get the stench of blood from her lungs. She turned on the shower and stripped off her clothes. She climbed in and let the hot water beat down on her. She scrubbed her hair and her body, wincing as her hands moved over the bruises made by the air bag. When she'd finished, she scrubbed her skin so roughly with the towel that it stung. She didn't care. By the time she dragged on a nightshirt, she was too exhausted to think. Her mind had had enough.

Hair still wet, she climbed beneath the covers and let the exhaustion consume her, dragging her into the darkness where the whispers she didn't understand waited.

She was running... Where was she? In the hall outside her room. Why was she running? The dark whispers followed her... April's voice, her laughter... The man whispering. Who was the man? David? Suddenly screams filled her ears. Who was screaming? Natalie was falling, falling, falling, and then her world went black.

Natalie bolted upright. Her frantic panting was the only sound in the darkness. More dreams. God. She pushed her still damp hair back from her face. Would this nightmare never end? The memory of the bloodstained clothes and the gun in her hamper slammed into her like a battering ram.

Soft laughter filled her mind...the whispers. April?

Knowing full well she was hearing things but unable to resist, Natalie threw back the covers and stormed out of the room, her anger and frustration building with every step. She marched straight to her sister's room and opened the door. The voices stopped the instant her gaze took in the empty room.

Natalie closed her eyes, took a deep breath and

exhaled slowly. What was happening to her? She was supposed to be getting better and stronger everyday.

A scream ripped through her ragged thoughts.

She ran to the staircase and stared down at the cold, unforgiving marble floor below...the place where she'd landed.

The screams...*her* screams...played over and over in her head making her dizzy.

Natalie hung on to the banister and lowered onto the top step. She pressed her hands to her ears and tried to quiet the screams. She couldn't bear it...didn't want to see.

"Natalie."

Someone was calling her name.

Hands clasped hers and pulled them away from her ears. Natalie opened her eyes. Clint stood over her, searching her face, his clouded with worry.

"You're okay. I'm here." He sat down beside her.

Tears spilled past her lashes despite her best efforts to hold them back. "I can't make it stop." He drew her into his arms. The feel of his warm skin and his strong arms ripped away the last of her defenses. "Please help me."

For a long moment he just held her. She cried against his shoulder, relished his warmth and strength. He drew her more firmly against him and stood. She wanted to protest as he carried her to her room. She could take care of herself. She'd always taken care of herself but somehow she had lost the ability. She needed help…she needed *him*.

He drew the covers back and lowered her to the bed and climbed in next to her. He pulled her against him and held her tight. He stroked her hair and whispered promises to her.

"I'll keep you safe. No one's going to hurt you now. I'm right here with you."

But how long would he stay when he learned her secret?

Friday, September 23, 6:30 a.m.

NATALIE'S EYES DRIFTED open and she turned her head to check the time. She had to get up. Get ready for work. Did she have court today?

Wait…memories came rushing back.

No court. She didn't even have a case. Not since the fall. Everything was different now.

Clint.

Heart starting to pound, she turned to check the other side of the bed. Empty. She smoothed her hand over the pillow, then pulled the sheet closer. The sheet still smelled like him. Warmth stirred deep inside her, but the sweet feeling was short-lived. She'd made a fool of herself last night with her nightmares and hallucinations.

When would they stop? She'd felt her life was

finally hers again until two months ago—when she started back to work. Was the pressure of merely showing up at the firm too much?

She didn't want to consider what kind of breakdown she would have if she dared to set foot in a courtroom.

"Stop." Natalie shook her head. She'd done the self-deprecating thing enough during her initial recovery. Going down that path now would be a big step backward. She had to stay focused on moving forward.

The memory of the bloody clothes and the gun jolted her.

She couldn't deal with that right now. At some point she would have to tell Clint, just not now. She couldn't do it yet. She couldn't bear the idea of him turning against her, too.

Moving quickly she selected a suit and the necessary underthings and hurried from the closet. Even with the bag closed up in the hamper the smell of blood seemed to assault her.

"It's only your imagination, Nat. Not real."

But the bloody clothes and the gun were all too real.

She stared at her reflection in the mirror. "You are a mess." Her hair was the most pressing matter at the moment. Going to bed with it wet was always a bad idea. Her chin still sported a red spot from the air bag. The bruising across her chest was a deeper blue. At least she was alive.

A snippet of memory—her frantically clutching at the railing and then falling. She swallowed back the fear and uncertainty that crowded into her throat. "Don't go there."

Half an hour later she looked reasonably calm and composed. Now for the hard part—facing Clint. She imagined he'd already decided she was in serious need of meds and more counseling. She'd fought so hard to get past that place. One step at a time she'd mastered the requirements for getting through a typical day. From dressing herself to making coffee and even driving again.

Was her brain determined to go in reverse now?

The smell of coffee had her forgetting her worries for a moment as she descended the stairs. In the kitchen she found Clint pouring freshly brewed coffee into two cups. His suit jacket hung over the back of a chair. The gray shirt and dark trousers fit his body as if they'd been tailored just for him. Judging by the man's closet she suspected that might very well be the case.

She summoned her courage and joined him at the counter to add cream to her coffee. "Good morning."

He glanced at her as he picked up his steaming mug. "Morning. You look well for a woman who battled an air bag just yesterday."

Not to mention her demons. She was grateful he didn't mention that part. Sadly, one of them had to clear the air. "I'm sorry about last night." She stared at her cup, watching the cream swirl into the dark Colombian roast.

"Did you remember something new?"

She shook her head and dared to meet his eyes. "I was dreaming, I suppose, about that night. The voices woke me and then I was at the stairs… falling."

"You screamed."

She looked away, embarrassed. "Sorry. They tell me I came out of the coma screaming. For months I would wake up screaming. I haven't done that in a really long time. Until…"

"Until you returned to work."

She nodded. "I guess Vince was right."

"Right about what?" he asked, his tone suddenly sharp.

Natalie searched Clint's face but he schooled his emotions before she could define what she saw. "When I first returned to the office he mentioned being worried that I was trying too much too soon."

"Don't trust him, Natalie. Take my word for it."

She wanted to ask if there was a personal history between the two of them but a call on his cell interrupted. Natalie took her coffee and wandered to the French doors that overlooked the gardens. She hoped it wasn't his friend Lieutenant Harper calling to tell Clint that he needed to arrest his new client for murder.

Natalie closed her eyes and sipped her coffee. Maybe she had imagined the bloody clothes. Except Suzanna had seen them, too. She should talk to Suzanna. How was she going to take care of this big old house without them? Granted she could understand they might truly want to retire, but she didn't want whatever was going on with her to be the reason.

This—whatever it was—had to stop.

When the call ended, she held her breath waiting for the news. From the corner of her eye she watched Clint sip his coffee. He wasn't looking forward to telling her the news. That much was clear.

Why didn't he just say it? They suspected her of shooting Beckett?

She opened her mouth to blurt the question but he spoke first. "The parking garage cameras didn't give us anything. We do know the gun used on Beckett was a .38."

"Like your father's," he didn't say. But she knew. Soon they would all know.

There was something terribly wrong with Natalie. The fall down those stairs had done far more damage than they had realized.

"I should get to the office."

She set her cup on the counter and walked out of the kitchen. She would be okay at the office. Work was the one thing that had never let her down—at least not that she could remember.

Richard Arrington Boulevard and 6th Avenue

NATALIE SAT FROZEN in the chair. Russ Brenner, Art Rosen and Peter Taylor sat on the other side of the conference table. Mr. Brenner's secretary had called Natalie into the conference room as soon as she arrived in the building. Clint had taken her briefcase and gone to wait in her office.

Brenner had kicked off the impromptu meeting with a lengthy monologue regarding Natalie's superior standing at the firm. Rosen had picked up from there, waxing on about how important the relationship with clients was to the continued success of the firm. Now, Taylor had taken his turn and launched into how the firm was like one big family. Somewhere along the way understanding had dawned on Natalie.

She was about to be fired.

"We care deeply for each member of our staff, especially our associates," Taylor went on. "However, we cannot afford the slightest risk to our clients. Our security protocols can never be anything less than impeccable."

"I do apologize," Natalie spoke up before he could continue, "but, with all due respect, I'm afraid I'm quite lost as to the point of this meeting."

The three exchanged a look. She wanted to pound her fist on the table and tell them to get to the damned point.

"Natalie," Rosen offered, "there has been a very serious breach in security. This morning we were informed that this breach originated from the computer in your office."

Horror tightened its grip around her throat. "Are you suggesting I had something to do with a security breach?" The idea was preposterous, but that was exactly what they were saying.

"We aren't accusing you of anything," Brenner put in quickly. "We are only saying that perhaps you aren't up to the stressors of the workplace. Perhaps you need more time off."

She was flabbergasted. "I don't know what to say. I thought my work since I returned had proven useful. I had hoped to be taking cases soon." She should have known better. Rather than her mental faculties improving, she was falling apart.

"You will always have a place here, Natalie," Rosen assured her. "We're suggesting that you take some more time and let's reevaluate in a few months."

"Months?" The rush of hurt and anger burned in her veins but Natalie refused to cause a scene. "Very well. If you believe that's best for the firm, then what else is there to say?" She stood. "Thank you so much. I'll make the necessary preparations for an extension of my leave."

"Give us a moment," Rosen said to the others.

Brenner and Taylor stood and shook her hand in turn.

When the room was theirs, Rosen came around to her side of the table and leaned against it. "Natalie, we've been through a lot together."

Every ounce of strength she possessed was required to hold back the words she wanted to hurl at him.

"You're well aware that you've always been my favorite."

Oh she was very well aware. *Deep breath, Nat.*

"But I have a responsibility to the other partners, to our clients and to the rest of the firm. You are not yourself. The accident changed you. When you're back to your old self, we'll make this right."

He dared to touch her, just a gentle brush of his cool fingers against her cheek. "Take care of yourself, Natalie. I'm going to miss you."

Shaking with fury, Natalie walked straight to

her office, feeling as if all eyes were on her. Clint stood as she entered the room. He took one look at her and opted not to ask the question she knew full well was poised on the tip of his tongue.

Rather than leave him in suspense, she said, "I've been asked to extend my leave from the firm. Apparently," she started to shove personal items into her briefcase, "there has been a security breach that originated from my computer and I've been deemed unreliable or untrustworthy— maybe both." She jammed in a few more items. "So, I'm on leave for a few more months."

He took the briefcase before she could attempt to stuff anything else into it, ensuring it never closed. "I'm certain it's only temporary."

"Maybe."

They exited her office. "Let's take the stairs." She had no desire to walk back down the hall past all those other office doors to reach the elevator.

Natalie held her tongue as they descended the stairs. She refused to be caught on the security cameras venting, which would only make bad matters worse.

"Natalie!"

Vince Farago hurried to catch up.

Natalie stopped and turned back to see what he had to say. She imagined he'd been gloating all morning. He was likely the first to hear the news.

"Are you all right?" he asked as he looked her

up and down and then glanced at Clint. "We're all very worried about you."

"I'm fine, Vince. I'll be taking a little more time off. There's no need for you to be concerned."

He glanced at Clint again. "I am concerned, Natalie. You haven't been yourself all week and… frankly, I have serious reservations about your involvement with Clint."

"I'll wait outside," Clint offered.

Natalie held up a hand. "No need." She lifted her gaze to Vince where he stood a few steps up. "I am fully aware of Clint's history and I have complete confidence in his ability. So, don't waste your time and energy worrying about me, Vince. I'm in very capable hands."

The bastard had the audacity to smirk. "I can't say I'm surprised. How long has it been since Steven dumped you? They say women get desperate after—"

Clint was nose to nose with him before Natalie realized he had moved.

"That's enough, Farago."

Vince held up his hands and backed away, almost stumbling on the step behind him. "Just telling it like I see it."

Clint turned his back on him and headed down the stairs, guiding Natalie along with him. The feel of his hand at the small of her back gave her a sense of reassurance she hadn't felt in a very long time.

Once they reached the parking garage, she paused before getting into the passenger seat of his Audi. "Thank you for backing me up."

The slow smile that released across his lips made her pulse flutter. "I'm the one who should thank you."

He had no idea. His only indiscretion was giving women what they wanted…she, on the other hand, had quite possibly killed a man.

She suddenly felt sick.

He squeezed her arm. "Don't worry. We've got this under control."

Natalie nodded and settled into the passenger seat. She should tell him what she'd found before he discovered the truth some other way. Her heart lurched. If she told him and he stopped believing in her, what would she do? Who could she trust?

The one thing she understood with complete certainty was that she could not do this alone.

Chapter Nine

Southwood Road
10:50 a.m.

Clint placed the last box on the dining room table. "Last one."

Rather than allow Natalie to stew over the injustice of the morning, he had decided to lay out his suspicions about her fall. In his opinion, it was someone from her professional life that had set out to harm or to kill her. If he'd had any doubts, the so-called security breaches on her computer at the firm had banished those.

Fortunately, Natalie kept copies of her work files at home. Going through those files, he decided, was a step in the right direction. Not to mention, he needed something more to do than to focus solely on the woman.

"Thanks." Natalie reached for the lid on the box. "This should be everything I need." She scanned the contents of the box before lifting her gaze back to his. "You really think what happened to me has something to do with the Thompson case?"

His fingers itched to reach out and brush those dark bangs back from her blue eyes. She had amazing blue eyes. Clear and inquisitive. Instead, he reached up and pulled the tie he'd already loosened free of his collar. His jacket lay across the sofa in the great room. He wished now that he'd brought something a bit more comfortable.

He cleared his head of any thoughts of getting more comfortable. He recognized the line to which he was edging far too close. "It's the only scenario that makes sense. Your accident took you off the defense team and suddenly the case does an about-face based on new evidence. Rison Medical gets the win and your colleague gets his long awaited spot in the limelight."

One hand on her hip, she rubbed her forehead with the other. "Vince isn't capable of…" Her voice trailed off. She turned to Clint. "Is he capable of pushing me down the stairs?"

"You were pushed?" Clint cocked an eyebrow at her question. He'd read all the reports related to her injury and never once did she or anyone else mention the possibility of her being pushed.

She shook her head and sighed. "I don't think so." She reached for a file. "Truth?"

He read the uncertainty in her eyes. "Nothing else will do."

"I don't know if I was pushed." She moistened her lips, drawing his hungry eyes there. "In my dreams, sometimes it feels like I'm being pushed, but it was dark and I just don't know for sure." She shook her head again. "The concept is ridiculous. No one was here with me except my sister. There is no way April pushed me."

The way she pretended to focus on the pages in the file belied her words. "You keep dreaming of hearing your sister in her room with a man. Are you sure her husband wasn't with her that night?"

"No, David was in Montgomery for a meeting. April said she called him from the hospital and let him know what happened."

It was time to take off the kid gloves. "Was she involved with someone else?"

"What?" Natalie's brow furrowed with a frown. "Of course not. April would never cheat on David."

Clint pulled out a chair and took a seat at the table. "Could Heath have been here with another woman that night?"

"Absolutely not." She tossed the file aside and moved on to the next one. "Heath is the quintessential good guy. He married his high school sweetheart. They go to church every Sunday and support every charity in Alabama. Their first child is on the way. No. Heath has always been the one who made April and me look like the bad children."

She assessed Clint for a moment. "Why all the questions about my siblings? I thought we cleared up any potential involvement by them when we first spoke?"

"You answer my questions and we won't go there again."

Her hesitation warned she wasn't happy. Still, she pulled out a chair and sat. Like his, her jacket was somewhere in the great room. Her heels were somewhere between here and there. If he'd been a stronger man he might not have watched her skirt slide up her thigh as she sat down, but he wasn't. He'd never wanted to be that strong.

"Fire away." She lifted her chin and waited for his first shot.

"What does either your sister or your brother have to gain if you were to die or be mentally incapacitated?"

She laughed, it was the first real laugh he'd heard from her. He liked it. The sound came from deep inside, making it rich and sweet.

"Well, that's easy." She lifted her arms wide apart. "This lovely old home that costs a mint to maintain. Fair market value is somewhere in the two-to three-million-dollar range. Since both my siblings have assets worth far more than the value of this estate, I highly doubt they're in any hurry to take it from me."

"Life insurance?"

She deliberated on her answer for a moment. "I have a healthy policy. Five million. Half of which goes to my siblings as long as I remain unmarried and the other half goes to my chosen charities."

Clint still wasn't convinced. "Are you protecting any family secrets?"

Natalie looked away. "I'm not sure what you mean."

So, she was covering up something. He leaned forward, braced his forearms on the table. "Do you have knowledge that could create problems for either of your siblings?"

"I do not." She grabbed another of the folders. "I thought we were going to discuss the Thompson case."

He would come back to this because the lady was definitely hiding something. "Walk me through the case."

"Walter Thompson entered the Rison Medical Center for a fairly routine procedure," Natalie began. "The complaint alleged that after his procedure the next morning, a nurse, Imogen Stuart, wheeled him back to his room and helped him to the bathroom, where he fell and hit his head. According to Stuart, Mr. Thompson did not fall until *after* she had settled him into his bed. Stuart claimed that as she was leaving the room he attempted to climb out of the bed to look for his wife and that was when he fell. The wife returned to the room as Stuart was helping him back into bed. So there were no witnesses to what actually happened. However it occured, the fall fractured his skull, causing an acute subdural hematoma that went undiagnosed until the onset of symptoms. He was rushed to surgery, but they were unable to save him. The wife insisted that her husband told her repeatedly that he'd fallen in the bathroom and that the nurse had been on her cell phone in the corridor instead of helping him."

"The nurse," Clint said, recalling the rumors he'd heard about the case, "stuck to her story that she never left Mr. Thompson's side until he was in the bed with the rails raised. Still, Rison offered to settle quietly but Thompson's wife insisted on a public admission of liability."

Natalie nodded. "She requested a jury trial. Except for her testimony, there was no evidence to support her allegations. An eleventh hour search of Mr. Thompson's health records—which had already been submitted as evidence—found a single incident of him falling down the garage steps when he knew better than to try going outside the house without assistance suggested a pattern that seemed to confirm Stuart's story and won the case."

"No one had noticed this incident before," Clint countered. Very convenient, in his opinion.

"It happens. You read files a hundred times and you miss a little something here or there. We were working night and day. It goes with the territory in a big case."

"There were rumors about a witness who confirmed the wife's allegations," Clint reminded her.

"Yes." Natalie reached for another folder in one of the boxes and took a moment to review it. "Just before trial Stuart claimed that her original statement was a mistake, but later she recanted that allegation." Natalie shook her head. "I don't remember any rumors about actual evidence."

"The timing of the rumors was around the same time you were recovering from your own fall."

"So that's why you asked about Vince." Natalie shrugged. "I can't see him going that far for a case—especially one that wasn't even his. You're thinking that if I hadn't fallen, I would have come forward with any evidence that might have damned my own client."

"Winning is more important than truth?"

She held up her hands stop-sign fashion. "You know as well as I do that I was bound by attorney-client privilege."

"As true as that is, I have a feeling you would never have ignored the truth."

She turned back to the files. "I appreciate your high opinion of me, but you must have forgotten the first rule of being an attorney."

"Never say never," he finished for her.

"It'll come back to bite you every time." Her lips lifted the slightest bit. "Most attorneys learn that lesson fast."

"What about your almost fiancé, Steven?" Clint had checked out the guy. Steven Vaughn was another politician. He'd been elected state representative the year before Natalie's accident. Vaughn and Keating, Natalie's brother-in-law, appeared to be close. If Clint's sources were accurate, Vaughn wanted to end up as lieutenant governor when Keating was elected to the state's highest position. Clint found it strange that Vaughn hadn't stuck by Natalie under the circumstances. Why hadn't Keating disassociated himself with Vaughn after he deserted Natalie? April had been all too happy to show her concern for her sister's association with Clint. Yet, she had no trouble with her husband maintaining close ties to the man who dumped her sister at the worst time in her life. It didn't sit right with Clint.

When Natalie continued to ignore the question, he nudged her again. "Was he in any way connected to the case?"

Natalie looked up. "I'm sorry. What was the question?"

"Never mind." Her distraction with one of the files from the box was more intriguing to him than anything she would likely tell him about the fiancé. "What're you reading?"

She frowned and turned her attention back to the file. "Stuart's statement is missing." She reached for the next file. "It's in here somewhere. I reviewed it with her before trial."

"Let's take it step by step." Clint surveyed the boxes he'd stacked on the table. "Where do we begin?"

"The day Rosen called me and two paralegals into the conference room." She pushed back her chair and went to one of the boxes stacked on the floor. "All we had was the incident report filled out by the hospital's head of security."

Clint moved to where she was opening the box. She lifted the first of several binders from the box. "Start here. I'll make tea."

He took the binder from her and watched her walk away.

Eventually she was going to have to share her secret with him.

NATALIE PLACED THE teakettle on the stove and adjusted the flame. She refused to think about the fact that she was now officially unemployed—no matter that the partners had insisted she would always have a place at the firm. She knew better. She needed to call Sadie and tell her.

Should she tell her about the gun and the bloody clothes, too?

Her hands shook and she almost dropped one of her grandmother's prized teacups. No. She wasn't telling anyone about that until she remembered why she had done such a thing.

"Like that's going to happen," she grumbled. She had no recall of blood on her clothes much less of changing and stashing the evidence. She'd been warned that unpleasant memories were the slowest to return.

She placed the cups and saucers on the counter and then reached for spoons. Clint made her want to trust him with that dark secret, but she wasn't sure she could even trust herself. How good were her instincts? Not very good now or before, she decided.

Steven had waited until she was out of the hospital and in rehab to break up with her. She'd wanted to be devastated, but she hadn't been. In all honesty, she hadn't been in love with him. At thirty years old she'd been more enamored with the idea of being engaged because all her friends were either engaged or married. April had kept pushing her to give Steven a chance.

Had she only committed to a serious relationship for appearances' sake or to make her sister and Steven happy?

Maybe so. From the time she was a young girl she'd wanted desperately to make the people around her happy. Her mother had scolded her time and again about being true to herself. Somehow it never took.

The kettle started to squeal, prompting her to gather tea bags.

Pounding from the front door reverberated in the entry hall. Natalie dropped the tea bags on the counter and started in that direction. Clint was already at the door and opening it.

Fear launched inside her. What if it was his police friends? Had they discovered the truth… that maybe she killed the mechanic?

Heath walked in, giving Clint a long, hard look as he passed him. "Nat, what the hell is going on here?"

She should have called her brother. April had obviously done so. "This is Clint Hayes." She accepted a kiss on the cheek from Heath. "Clint, this is my brother, Heath." Heath was older than she by one year and taller by about a foot. He was a big, broad-shouldered guy and he'd always considered himself the protector of his sisters.

The two men shook hands, but the gesture was quick and visibly unfriendly.

"Clint is the private investigator helping me sort out the strange happenings of late."

Heath stared at Clint, openly skeptical. "April said he was some kind of gigolo out for your money."

Natalie laughed, couldn't help herself. "Trust me, big brother, Clint doesn't need my money."

Clint's stony features warned that he wasn't amused.

Heath grinned. "April's always been a drama queen. Besides," he looked Clint up and down, "if he makes you happy I don't care what he is. I never liked Steven, he had his nose too far up David's—"

"I know what you think of Steven," Natalie cut in. "We were about to have tea. Would you like some?"

"Tea's for old ladies," Heath grumbled as they moved into the kitchen.

"Be nice," Natalie warned. Heath had snubbed his nose at college, choosing instead to immerse himself in the family business. Who needed a college degree to know how to manufacture steel, he'd said. So proud of his only son, their father had indulged him for a little while. Eventually he and Heath had struck a deal. Heath continued at the plant by day and attended college classes in the evening. An MBA hadn't changed her brother much. He was still the man who was as happy working alongside a manual laborer as he was behind a desk. The degree, however, had made their father very happy. Natalie inserted a pod into the coffee machine to brew her brother a cup.

"You were a cop before becoming a PI?" Heath asked as he and Clint settled at the breakfast table.

"That's right," Clint confirmed.

Heath grunted. "You went to law school, too, I hear."

"I did."

"Heath," Natalie sent him a warning look as she poured the tea, "do not embarrass me or yourself."

"I don't blame him for changing his mind. Lawyers—" he glanced at his sister "—my sister not included, are a pain in the butt."

She placed the cup of coffee in front of him and sent him a disapproving look.

"They are a different breed," Clint agreed.

With tea and coffee served, Natalie joined them at the table.

"April says Suzanna and Leonard quit."

Suzanna's words echoed inside Natalie. "I suppose it was time they retired."

"Seems strange to me."

"I find it strange," Clint said, "that you were at the BMW dealership this week and a mechanic there, Mike Beckett, tampered with Natalie's car."

Natalie started to demand what Clint was

thinking when Heath looked from Clint to her. "Is he serious?"

"I am," Clint answered. "Someone tampered with the air bag in Natalie's car. She could have been killed in the crash."

"You crashed your car?" Heath threw up his hands. "Nobody ever tells me anything."

She and Clint would talk later. For now Natalie kept her temper in check. "The air bag launched and I crashed into a car in a parking lot. No one was hurt. Other than the few bruises and a couple of abrasions I sustained."

Heath shifted his attention back to Clint. "You're sure it wasn't just a factory malfunction."

"It was no malfunction."

Heath scrubbed a hand over his face. "Well, then, I guess I should have paid more attention to the bastard is all I can say."

"What do you mean?" Natalie's heart nearly stopped. How could Heath know anything about this?

"The knucklehead called me a few days ago and said you were going to get hurt but he could stop it from happening for the right price."

"That's why you went to see him?" Clint pressed.

Heath nodded. "Only he wasn't there. The shop foreman said Beckett had been off all week. Some kind of family emergency. I thought he was a nutcase but I wasn't going to risk Nat's safety so I went to see him, yeah. Did the cops arrest him?"

Natalie couldn't breathe. She clasped her hands in her lap so no one could see them shake.

"He was found at home yesterday," Clint told him. "Murdered."

"Damn." Heath turned to Natalie again. "What's going on, Nat? Why the hell didn't you tell me about this?"

She shook her head, not trusting her voice.

"We believe," Clint said, drawing his attention, "someone hired Beckett to tamper with the air bag and then maybe that same person silenced him."

"This doesn't make sense." Heath pushed away his coffee. "Who would want to hurt you? You haven't been getting those threatening letters again, have you?"

Shock radiated through Natalie. "What?"

"Remember? About two weeks before your accident you started getting these letters. You know," he glanced at Clint, "the kind done with words cut out of a magazine or newspaper and then glued on the page. I was here when you opened the second one. You promised to call the cops, but I don't think you did. Then everything happened and I forgot about it until just now. You made me promise not to tell anyone. You thought it was about that damned case."

"Thompson versus Rison Medical?" Clint asked.

"Yeah, that's the one."

The image of a page with cut and pasted words swam before her eyes. *I know the truth, do you?* A few days later a second one had come. *Are you really going to let this happen?*

"I never got the chance to call the police." The words were scarcely a whisper. She had been very upset by the letters because she knew what they meant…she had known something then that eluded her now.

Why couldn't she remember what it meant? What truth?

Clint's voice as he answered his cell dragged her away from the troubling thoughts.

"I understand." He ended the call and put his phone away. "We need to speak privately."

Heath stood. "I have to get back to the plant."

Natalie managed to get to her feet without swaying. "I'm glad you came by." She loved her family. She wished they had more time together. Though April had spent most nights with her for months, they never really talked the way they used to.

After she had assured Heath she would keep him informed and shown him out, she turned to the man waiting in the middle of the entry hall. Judging by the grim face he wore, the news wasn't good.

"Beckett's girlfriend claims he was blackmailing someone about *you*. The morning he was murdered he was supposed to meet with that person. Harper and Cook are on their way here. Is there anything you want to tell me before they arrive?"

Ice chilled Natalie's veins. "There's something in my closet you need to see."

Chapter Ten

Clint waited at the door while Natalie crossed to the far side of her walk-in closet. She stared at a wicker laundry hamper for a moment before opening it. The little gasp that followed had him moving toward her.

She reached into the hamper and then drew back, her expression somewhere between shock and fear. "It's gone."

"What's gone?" He peered into the empty hamper.

"The gun." She met his gaze. "Yesterday Suzanna told me she'd found a gun and bloody clothes in my room and that she couldn't protect me anymore. I had no idea what she meant, and then last night I found a white garbage bag in the hamper." She closed her eyes and shook her head.

"You're thinking the clothes and gun were from when you shot the intruder."

"Except the gun disappeared along with the intruder." She stared into the empty hamper again. "How could I not remember changing clothes and hiding the gun before calling the police? My brain tells me that I ran out of the house and called 9-1-1."

The doorbell rang, echoing through the house. Natalie looked stricken.

"Is there anything else you haven't told me? Anything at all?" Clint might be a sucker but he believed her. She needed to be straight with him. Any secrets she held back could create serious problems going forward. With a man dead, this was no time to hold back.

"I think my sister *was* having an affair." Natalie let go a shaky breath. "My brain keeps replaying these voices and this soft laugher. One of the voices belongs to April, the other to a man. The voices wake me up and I follow the sounds to April's bedroom—the one she slept in growing up and uses whenever she stays the night. For the past several weeks it's happened every night. No one's there, of course, but it has to mean something. Once the voices wake me up, I go to the stairs and I remember snippets of my fall."

Clint braced his hands on his hips and contemplated the possibilities. "Why do you think that means she's having an affair? Maybe her husband was here with her."

Natalie hugged her arms around herself. "I've

tried to convince myself the male voice was her husband's, but in my heart I know that's not true. David and I were never really friends. He certainly wouldn't have spent the night here. Frankly, at the time, April wouldn't have either unless she and David had quarreled."

Clint nodded. "All right."

The doorbell sounded again. She flinched.

"For now we keep this between us." No need to put her through the kind of interrogation associated with being a suspect in a homicide until they sorted out what the hell was going on around here.

"It's bad enough that I've impeded the investigation into the intruder I'm certain I shot," she protested. "I can't have you breaking the law for me by doing the same in a homicide investigation. This has gone too far already, Clint."

"Let me worry about the homicide investigation." He had no intention of hindering anything. "We shouldn't keep them waiting."

The doorbell launched into its classic tune a third time before Clint reached the door. Natalie waited in the great room. She needed a moment to pull herself together. He sure as hell hoped she wasn't holding back anything else.

He opened the door as Harper was calling his cell. Harper ended the call and dropped his phone back into the pocket of his suit jacket. "Everything okay?"

Anytime a person of interest knew the police were en route and took his time getting to the door it created suspicion.

"Besides a dead mechanic who tampered with my client's car?" Clint gestured for the two detectives to enter. "Everything is just peachy."

Harper sent him a sidelong glance. "Where's Ms. Drummond?"

Clint ignored Harper's skeptical tone. The man was always overly suspicious when it came to murder. "This way."

As they joined her in the great room, Natalie summoned a faint smile. Clint wished he could take some of the worry off her shoulders. So far he was batting zero where her peace of mind was concerned.

"Lieutenant Harper and Detective Cook are here about the mechanic who may have tampered with your car," Clint explained.

"Ms. Drummond." Harper nodded as he took a seat on the sofa across from where she sat. "I'm sorry to bother you with more questions, but unfortunately it's necessary."

"I understand."

Natalie was nervous. Harper would notice. Natalie had tried a number of high-profile cases. The idea of the woman who'd come so close to being the youngest partner in such a prestigious firm being nervous under any circumstances was completely out of character.

Spending as much time with her as he had the past few days, Clint got it. The brain injury had done a number on her and her confidence in herself. A great deal of what an attorney did relied completely upon the ability to recall and analyze the facts as well as the law. The injury had taken away, at least to some degree, her ability to recall facts as well as the sequence of past events. How could she assess the problem if parts were missing or out of order? She had every right to be nervous and uncertain. Someone was taking advantage of her vulnerability.

As Harper started his questions, Cook took his cue from Clint and opted to stand. The young detective had chosen Clint as his role model. Clint had tried repeatedly to discourage him, but he was one determined guy. Clint liked him, as well. Shortly after joining the BPD's Special Problems Unit, he'd helped Cook prepare for the detective's exam. They'd been friends since.

The team had formed a strong bond—one carried beyond the job. They were like family.

"Ma'am, you stated that when the intruder entered your home you took the .38 that belonged to your father and fired it at him."

Clint's attention shifted back to Natalie. She nodded. "That's correct."

"You dropped the weapon, left the intruder wounded and ran from the house to call the police?"

"Yes. I might have reacted differently in the past," she admitted. "The TBI altered certain things about my personality, at least for now."

"You believe the intruder took the weapon and left while you were waiting outside for the police?"

"I do, yes."

She relaxed a bit. Clint did the same.

"Where on your property did you wait? Were you near the house?" Harper asked.

"No." She shook her head emphatically. "I waited in the street. I was terrified. I even knocked on the front door of my closest neighbor, but no one was home."

Clint had read the report. She hadn't mentioned going to the neighbor's house in her initial statement. If she was remembering more details, that was a good thing. If she was confusing the facts, that was not. He hoped the former was the case. If Harper didn't mention the point, Clint would. Later.

Harper flipped back through the pages of his notepad. Clearly he'd picked up on the discrepancy. "You didn't mention going to the neighbor's house in your statement."

Natalie frowned. "I was upset. I must have forgotten to mention it. No one was home so it wasn't relevant."

Harper scratched a few words on his notepad. "Your father owned a Smith & Wesson .38. That's the weapon you used on the intruder?"

"Yes. My father owned it for as long as I can remember. I suppose I should have registered it in my name after his death. I simply never got around to it."

"Had you fired the weapon before?"

"No." She glanced at Clint for the first time. Her tension rising again. "I took a course on weapon safety after I inherited the house and the gun, but other than the course and the intruder, I've never fired any weapon."

"Ma'am, did Lieutenant Russell have someone swab your hand for gun powder residue?"

"No. He didn't believe there had been an intruder or a gun. I didn't think of that myself until days later or I would have insisted the test be done."

Tension nudging him, Clint moved to stand behind Natalie. "Where is this going, Harper?"

"The slug removed from Beckett's chest was a .38," Harper said, his face somber. "The ballistics was an exact match to the slug we recovered from the trash in his bathroom where he'd tended his first gunshot wound. The one we believe he sustained here."

Natalie's hand went to her throat as she looked over her shoulder at Clint.

"I thought Beckett died from a single gunshot wound to the chest," Clint argued. "How did you miss the second gunshot?"

"The shot to the chest is what killed him," Harper said. "He'd already patched up the other wound and changed clothes. We didn't know about it until we found the evidence of the cleanup in the bathroom. I called the ME's office and got confirmation about the second wound."

Natalie said, "Wait, are you saying the weapon taken from my home was used to kill him?"

"Yes, ma'am."

"Did you recover the weapon?" Clint asked, his own tension ramping up. If the housekeeper found the .38 here and Natalie saw it just last night, how the hell could it be the same weapon?

Harper shook his head. "The shooter took it with him…or *her*."

"The ME estimated time of death at what time?" Clint knew damn well Harper had that piece of information. For whatever reason he'd chosen not to share it up front.

"Between nine and midnight on Wednesday night." Harper turned his attention back to Natalie. "Ma'am, have you ever had any dealings with Beckett beyond having your personal vehicle serviced at the shop where he worked?"

She shook her head. "I didn't know his name before this… and to my knowledge I never met him."

"Does anyone else in your family or a close friend use that dealership?"

"The manager said my brother had bought a car there for his wife. I'm not aware of anyone else using it. My sister and her husband prefer Mercedes."

Harper closed his notepad and stuffed it back into his jacket pocket. "Ma'am, if you think of anything else that might help our investigation, Hayes knows how to reach me."

The pointless meeting ended and Clint escorted the two detectives to the door. "You could have asked those questions when you called."

Harper shrugged. "Then I wouldn't have seen her reaction. She's hiding something, my friend. And you know it."

"Since I was here with her all night Wednesday night, we know she's not your shooter."

"I never thought she was," Harper admitted. "But this guy had a connection to her or to someone close to her."

"Did you find evidence at the scene or are you going solely on the girlfriend's testimony?

We both know emotional witnesses are rarely good ones."

"Watch your back, Hayes," Harper warned. "Something's up with this family."

Cook kept his head down as he followed the senior detective out the door.

Yeah, well, Clint was well aware that the Drummonds had more secrets than they wanted to share.

Who didn't have secrets?

NATALIE STOOD AT the window watching the two detectives leave. The man she'd shot was dead. Her father's gun had been used to shoot him a second time. The same bloodstained gun she had seen in her laundry hamper last night.

Clint joined her at the window. "I was here with you when Beckett was murdered. Whatever you're thinking, you had nothing to do with his death."

"Someone close to me did." Emotion swelled into her throat. How could she believe her sister or her brother had done this? April was the one behaving so irrationally, but it was Heath who had gone to the dealership looking for Beckett. He was the one Beckett had contacted with a blackmail threat.

She closed her eyes. Why would Beckett or

anyone else want to hurt her? What had she done to make anyone that angry?

"I can think of only two reasons anyone would want you out of the way, Natalie. You're either standing in the way of something or you know something they want to hide."

He said the words softly but there was nothing soft about the meaning. "I know. I just can't remember what it is."

"We will find the answer."

"I don't want anyone else to end up dead." She turned to face him. "If my sister or my brother are somehow involved or if they're targets, too…" She closed her eyes and struggled to slow the emotions whirling inside her. Somewhere on this journey she lost the ability to keep her wits about her.

Warm fingers brushed her cheek, stealing her breath and at the same time soothing her frayed nerves. She opened her eyes and searched his as he spoke. "We should have a meeting with your family and warn them about the situation."

She forced the softer emotions aside and gave him a skeptical look. "Warn them or assess their reaction to what we know so far?"

"Both. We should talk to Suzanna and Leonard, as well. Suzanna may know more than she's told you."

"She said she couldn't protect me anymore. I don't know what that means."

"We'll find out. I'm certain you're skilled in how to approach a hostile witness."

Natalie thought of the way April had behaved and then Suzanna's abrupt departure. And even Heath's unexpected visit. "I guess I never expected the hostile witness to be a member of my family."

"Sometimes family is the most hostile of all."

She searched his face. As silly as it was, she had memorized every line and angle. His eyes were the part that tugged at her the most, so very dark and tempting. His eyes made her want to be closer…to know him more intimately. If only she dared permit herself to indulge in those feelings again. A relationship required trust. She didn't trust herself—how could she expect anyone else to have faith in her?

"You don't doubt me, do you?" she asked. His answer was suddenly, inexplicably important to her.

"I believe you've told me everything you feel is relevant."

"You're evading the question, counselor." She wanted him to trust her. No, she needed him to… at least on some level.

"You hold back what you're unsure about. I need you to trust me with your darkest secrets,

Natalie. You're aware of how important full disclosure is to any case."

There was certainly no denying that charge. "The only things I haven't told you are the vague images I see in my dreams or hallucinations. At first it was nothing more than pages of briefs or reports. The words fall from the pages into a pile before igniting. It wasn't until after Heath mentioned the threatening letters that I remembered receiving them. Typically that's the way it works. If a memory is triggered it comes to the surface. Otherwise it just stays buried somewhere in my gray matter."

"You remembered nothing about the cut-and-paste letters until your brother mentioned them?"

"Nothing." She wanted to scream in frustration. "As soon as he mentioned them pieces of memories returned. I could see the letters. One said something like 'I know the truth, do you?' There was another that demanded how I was going to let this happen. If there's more, I can't remember them."

He held her gaze but said nothing. What was there to say? Her dreams made no sense. The way the memories returned was unreliable at best.

Finally she had to look away. "I don't know how I thought I could practice law again." She closed her eyes and shook her head, then took a breath and dared to meet his steady gaze once more. "Sorry. I'm usually a little stronger than this."

"You're plenty strong, Natalie."

Why oh why did he have to look at her that way? As if he appreciated what he saw…as if he wanted more than to talk.

"Would you just…" Good grief, what was she thinking? She looked away.

He took her face in his hands and turned her eyes to his. "I would."

Her next breath deserted her as his lips lowered to hers. He brushed her mouth with his so very softly once, twice and then he kissed her slow, deep and deeper still. She leaned against him, relishing the feel of his warm body.

His fingers delved into her hair, angling her head just so to deepen the kiss.

And then he stopped. Every part of her protested. He pressed his forehead to hers. "We have work to do."

She licked her lips, savored the taste of him. "Yes."

For once, she wished he was wrong.

Chapter Eleven

Wenonah Road
2:00 p.m.

Clint parked at the curb in front of the house belonging to Imogene Stuart. "You do understand this is crossing a line. The firm will fire you for a move like this."

She nodded. "For all intents and purposes, they've already fired me."

"There will be damage to your professional reputation," he reminded her.

She turned to him. "I have to do this. I *need* to know."

He nodded. "I can do this part without you. You don't have to—"

Natalie placed her hand on his arm. "I need to do this."

Clint emerged from the car and went around to the passenger side to meet her. His instincts moved to the next level. He took a long look around the neighborhood. He didn't see anything that looked out of place, but he felt it.

They were being watched.

Narrowing his focus, he scanned for any sign of a dog. The home was a small bungalow from the first quarter of the last century, bordered by a neat yard and a picket fence in need of a fresh coat of paint. A quick search had shown that Imogene's husband passed away less than a week before the Thompson-Rison Medical trial. The twenty-year-old Dodge parked on the street was registered to the owner of the house, which hopefully meant she was home.

He climbed the steps behind Natalie, keeping an eye out for whoever was watching them as well as for a dog. He liked dogs but they often didn't like him. As a cop he'd run into more than his share of unfriendly ones. There was always the chance that perps trained their dogs to dislike cops on sight. Maybe he'd have better luck as a private investigator.

Natalie opened the wooden screen door and knocked.

Television noise suggested someone was at home. The curtain in the window to the left of the door moved just enough for the occupant to have a look. It paid to be careful these days, particularly for a woman at home alone.

The door opened a crack. "No solicitors." Female. Brown hair streaked with gray and a pair of glasses that shielded accusing eyes glared at them.

Clint gifted the lady with a smile. "We're not solicitors, ma'am. We need a few minutes of your time to—"

"I have my own church, so just take it on next door. The heathens who live there could do with a sermon."

Natalie said, "Mrs. Stuart, my name is—"

"Wait." The door opened a fraction farther. The older woman scrutinized Natalie a bit more closely. "I know who you are." Her lips tightened in anger, then she said, "I have nothing else to stay to you."

When the door would have closed, Natalie braced a hand against it and stuck her foot in its way. "Please, Mrs. Stuart. This is very important."

Whether the lady of the house allowed them in or not, Clint was impressed. This was the side of Natalie Drummond that had gone dormant with the brain injury. He was glad to see a glimmer of the fighter she used to be.

The door opened wide. "I'll hear what you have to say because I'm a Christian. Come on in." Stuart turned her back and shuffled to the sofa.

Natalie exchanged a look with him before

going inside. Clint followed, closing the door behind him.

"Thank you, Mrs. Stuart. This is—"

"Clint Hayes." He extended his hand to the lady. "It's a pleasure to meet you, ma'am."

Openly suspicious, she accepted the offered hand and gave it a shake. "We'll see about that."

He smiled. "I suppose we will."

"Take a seat." She reached for the remote and muted the television.

Clint waited for Natalie to be seated first, and then he took the remaining chair.

"Mrs. Stuart, I'd like to ask you a few questions about the Thompson case."

Stuart had a kind face but there was nothing kind about the fury that contorted her features just then. "Why would you come back here now? It's done. I told you all I had to say the last time we talked."

Clint watched Natalie's face. She seemed surprised at the woman's words.

"I was on the legal team for your employer, I'm sure we spoke many times, Mrs. Stuart."

Stuart's gaze narrowed behind her glasses. "I'm talking about the private conversation we had. The one where I answered a certain question you had asked me."

"I don't understand," Natalie pressed. "What private conversation?"

Stuart got to her feet. "I don't know what you think you're doing, but I'm not going to jail for what I was forced to do by your firm so you just get out of my house right now."

"Please," Natalie kept her seat, "let me explain."

Clint kept quiet. If he got involved at this point Stuart would likely feel pressured.

Openly reluctant, Stuart took her seat once more.

"Before the trial I was injured." Natalie gestured to her head. "A brain injury. I was in the hospital for weeks and then in rehab for months after that. I've only recently started to work again."

Gaze still narrowed in suspicion, Stuart asked, "Is that why I didn't see you at the trial? I kept expecting you to do something. But I never saw you again after we talked."

A cold, sick feeling twisted in Clint's gut.

"Yes. I was in the hospital fighting for my life."

Stuart's face softened. "I didn't know. I just figured they shut you up the way they did the rest of us."

Natalie glanced at Clint. The worry on her face told him all he needed to know. She wasn't sure what was coming and she was terrified it would be news she didn't want to hear.

"Can you tell me what question I asked?"

"Don't see why I can't." Stuart took a big

breath. "You asked if anyone instructed me to change my story about what happened in Mr. Thompson's room that morning."

Natalie waited for a long moment before she responded. "Will you share your answer with me again?"

Stuart shook her head. "No way. They made me sign one of those papers that says I can never talk about it again." She frowned. "You can't remember?"

Natalie shook her head. "I'm sorry. I don't remember."

Stuart nodded. "That's a real shame." She stood once more. "I wish I could help you, but I'm all alone now. As you know I lost my husband to cancer. His treatments took a lot of money. My retirement from Rison Medical is all I got. I can't risk losing it or having them come after me in a lawsuit." She took a big breath as if trying to shore up her courage. "You should leave now and don't come back."

Natalie stood. Clint did the same. Stuart was afraid to talk and he got that. Anything she did or said posed great risk to her livelihood. If his theory about what happened to Natalie was correct, Stuart's life could be in danger, as well.

Natalie hesitated at the door. "Mrs. Stuart, is there anything at all you can say that might guide me in my search for what really happened."

Stuart hesitated for only a few seconds. "Look at the evidence you have. That will tell you all you need to know. You had it before the trial, maybe you still do."

"I don't have any evidence beyond what you saw presented at trial."

"Yes you do. I gave it to you." She shook her head, "I tried to tell you with those anonymous letters warning you to do something, and then I called. After that we met in person and I gave you what you needed to make things right. I did all I could do two years ago. I can't help you now."

Stuart ushered them onto the porch and closed her door.

"At least now we know who sent the cut-and-paste letters," Natalie said wearily.

"That's something." Clint scanned the street. Coming here may have been a mistake. If this was where Natalie had come just before her fall…then whatever it was she'd been told at the time was why she ended up at the bottom of those stairs.

Moss Rose Lane
Hoover
5:15 p.m.

"THIS IS TOO RISKY."

Natalie reached for patience. Clint wanted her to stay at his office with Jess but she couldn't do that. "We can't be sure she'll even talk to me," she argued. "I won't risk scaring her off with a stranger."

Clint stared out the windshield of his Audi, his profile turning to stone. He'd told her he suspected they were being watched but he hadn't spotted a tail since leaving the Stuart home. Natalie wanted to hope he'd been wrong about their being watched, but she felt confident his instincts were far too good for such a mistake.

"No memories were triggered when I was at Mrs. Stuart's home," she urged when he remained silent. "That's not a good sign, Clint. It means those memories may be lost forever. If there's no chance of my recalling what she's talking about, I have to find it another way. This—Mrs. Thompson—is the way. Maybe the only way."

He turned to her, his dark eyes nearly black with frustration or something on that order. "They are watching us."

"You can't be sure. You said you hadn't seen—"

"You worked at your firm for four years before your injury, you are well aware of how smart and cunning those guys are. Whether we spot their eyes or not, they *are* watching us."

He was right. There was no point in denying the assertion or his perceptive skills. She supposed she should be afraid but somehow she wasn't. She was out of a job anyway, but if any-one at her firm was responsible for her fall…

Natalie couldn't assimilate the concept just now. Seeing this investigation through required all her cognitive skills. "Let's give them some-thing to worry about."

Before he could argue, she opened the door and got out. She surveyed the street, giving who-ever was watching a perfect view of her face no matter where they were hiding. Clint slammed his door, darting a hard look in her direction. He recognized exactly what she'd done.

Mrs. Thompson lived in the same home she had shared with her husband. A classic brick ranch with a big yard and perfectly manicured shrubs. Natalie was halfway up the sidewalk when a big dog raced around the corner of the house, barking for all it was worth.

She froze. Clint stepped in front of her. "Good boy."

The dog obviously didn't feel the same. He growled.

Clint crouched down and offered his hand, palm down.

"Do you think that's a good idea?" Natalie held her breath as the dog she now recognized as a golden retriever eased closer to Clint.

"You're just protecting your kingdom, aren't you boy?"

"Jasper!"

Natalie looked up. Mrs. Thompson stood at the front door. She produced the biggest smile she could manage and waved to the woman. "Mrs. Thompson, it's Natalie Drummond."

The dog trotted up the two steps onto the porch. Clint pushed to his feet and started that way. Natalie moved up beside him, hoping Thompson wouldn't shut the door in their faces.

Watching their approach, Thompson scratched Jasper behind the ears. "I remember you. You're one of those lawyers who cheated me and my family out of what we deserved."

Natalie would have preferred to deny the charge. Instead, she crossed the porch and stood before her accuser. "I guess I am. This is Clint Hayes, my associate." Natalie didn't want to frighten her by mentioning the term *private investigator*.

Thompson glanced at Clint. "What do you want?"

As if a gust of cold wind had swept through her soul, Natalie remembered the devastated wife during her deposition. The images and the voices poured through her, stealing her breath and at the same time sending her heart pounding. She and her husband had been married for twenty-five years. Being a wife and mother was all she had ever known. She had three children in college at the time, ranging from a freshman to a senior. The whole family had been devastated. Natalie felt ill at the idea that she may have been a party to compounding that devastation.

Summoning her wits, Natalie said, "I want to know what really happened in that hospital room."

Rather than startle Thompson as Natalie had thought the statement would, it seemed to enrage her. "How dare you come back here after two years and stir that pot again. I told you the last time you stood on my porch what really happened and you promised to make sure the truth came out in that courtroom." She shook her head. "I don't know what your game is, lady, but I want you off my property. Now."

Natalie's knees felt weak. "You're saying I came to your home before the trial and discussed the case with you?" That alone was a career-killing move.

"You damned sure did."

As if sensing the shift in the tension, Jasper growled. His mistress called him down.

"Mrs. Thompson, can you tell me the exact date I came to your home?" Natalie's pulse raced, her heart pounded so hard she could scarcely hear herself think over the roar of her own blood.

Thompson's gaze narrowed. "Something happened to you, didn't it? I remember seeing you on the news."

Natalie nodded. "I was in the hospital for a long time." She had no desire to discuss her injury a second time today.

Thompson ushered her dog inside. "Come on in and I'll look it up." She went on as they followed her into the house, "I think it was the day before the trial. I even told my lawyer but I don't think he believed me since you never returned any of his calls."

She gestured to the sofa. "Sit. I'll get my calendar."

Natalie and Clint settled on the sofa. He appeared focused on taking in the details of the room. Mrs. Thompson's walls were filled with family photos. A portrait of her husband was centered on the wall above the television. A cross hung on one side of the portrait and an angel hung on the other. Natalie's heart pressed harder against her sternum, threatening to burst from her chest.

"Here we go." Thompson came back into the room carrying a standard wall calendar. She sat down in what Natalie suspected was her favorite chair and flipped through the pages. "So…" She studied the page. "You came on Sunday around five o'clock the evening before the trial."

She passed the calendar across the coffee table.

Natalie, hand trembling, accepted it. She looked over the page and all the notes Thompson had scribbled on the blocks that represented days in that month. Her throat tightened when she read her name penciled in as Thompson had said.

With monumental effort, Natalie returned the calendar to its owner.

"Will you tell us what you and Ms. Drummond discussed that day?"

Thompson shifted her suspicious gaze to Clint. "She wanted me to repeat what happened to my husband. I told her, same thing I told everyone who asked because it was the truth. After his procedure, I stopped by the cafeteria for coffee and a breakfast sandwich. The nurse was supposed to be taking care of my husband. She was supposed to get him back to the room and into bed."

She paused a moment, the memories visibly painful. "My husband said he told her he needed to go to the bathroom. She helped him to the toilet but then she got a call on her cell. He kept waiting for her to come back but she didn't so he got up and tried to get to bed on his own. He fell in the bathroom and hit his head on the shower curb. I guess she must have heard him because she rushed in there and helped him up and to the bed. When I walked in he was talking and seemed to be okay so the nurse didn't act worried."

The lucid interval. The death of actor Liam

Neeson's wife had made the term a household one. Thompson had repeatedly mentioned what she'd seen on television and read in magazines and, she claimed, the staff ignored her.

"They killed him. Not only did the nurse let him fall, they ignored my concerns about checking his head with an MRI or something until it was too late."

"Mrs. Thompson, did I say anything to you the day I came to your home that made you believe I possessed knowledge or evidence that confirmed your allegations?"

Clint sent Natalie a questioning look. He didn't have to say a word. With that question she had crossed the point of no return. She had just implicated herself in a possible fraudulent act—not to mention she'd broken attorney-client privilege.

"You said for me not to worry, you were going to make it right."

And that night she had fallen down the stairs.

Chapter Twelve

Lori Wells joined them at the dining room table. "Sorry about that, guys. Layla should sleep for a while now."

"Your little girl is beautiful," Natalie said.

Lori beamed. "Thank you. We think so."

"I hear you're still working too many hours," Clint said as Lori grabbed her beer.

"Don't get him started." Lori darted a look at her husband.

Harper had made lieutenant only a few months ago. With Jess and Clint gone, Harper was the senior detective in SPU, the major crimes team. Lori had moved over to Crimes Against Persons.

Chet Harper grunted as he glanced up from the

report he was reviewing. "Her mom takes good care of Layla when we're at work."

Lori grinned. "Sounds like someone's trying to stay on my good side tonight."

Clint laughed. "The joys of married life."

"And how would you know, Mr. I'm-staying-single-forever?" Lori teased.

Clint held up his hands surrender style. "You've got me there."

Lori turned to Natalie. "I do have wine if you'd prefer."

Natalie had accepted the offer of a beer but she'd hardly touched it. "No thanks. The beer is fine." She lifted the bottle to her lips as if to confirm her words.

Harper closed the folder in front of him and reached for another. "The case reads pretty cut-and-dried." He glanced up at Clint. "It boiled down to the word of the nurse against the wife."

"Why didn't she take the settlement they offered instead of going to trial?" Lori asked. "Seems like that would have saved her a lot of grief."

"Mrs. Thompson really wanted the world to know what Rison had done," Natalie spoke up. "Her attorney was adamant that the only way to do that was a trial. I'm sure you're aware the settlement offer would have come with a confidentiality agreement."

Lori made a face. "Wow. She risked everything to try to get justice for her husband."

Natalie nodded slowly. "Others would see it as an attempt to get more money."

"Lawyers." Harper looked from Natalie to Clint and back. "No offense, ma'am. Sometimes I wonder…"

"If we have hearts?" she finished for him. "Sometimes it feels as if we don't, but everyone has a job to do. Keep in mind there are plenty of unethical people out there who file lawsuits based on false claims."

Lori rolled her eyes. "Forgive my husband. He sometimes speaks before thinking."

Clint laughed. "I thought I was the one who had that problem."

"You are," Harper assured him.

They all had a good laugh, but the amusement died quickly.

"Natalie," Lori broached the bottom line first, "it's pretty clear from an investigator's point of view that your accident was no accident. I'm with Clint on this one. I think it has to do with the Thompson case, which means someone at your firm could very well be responsible."

Clint wished there were a different answer, but he couldn't see any other scenario. He added, "You know the only alternative."

Natalie inhaled a deep breath. "My family."

She moved her head from side to side. "For all our imperfections, we love each other. I don't believe my family was involved."

"The firm won't let this go," Clint reminded her. "I'm certain they have someone watching us."

"Unfortunately," Natalie confessed, "I have to agree."

"Our next step is to determine who has the most to lose if you recall whatever it was Stuart confided in you." Lori scooted the files over to one side and unearthed a sheet of poster board. She grabbed a marker. "Where would you start?"

"Vince Farago," Clint answered for her. "He wanted to be partner. Natalie was under consideration before her fall. He stepped into her spot on the team defending Rison."

Natalie didn't disagree with him. Maybe she finally recognized Farago for what he was—a shark with a straightforward motto: eat, sleep, kill.

Lori added his name to the board. "Anyone else?"

Natalie leaned forward and braced her arms on the table. "There's one other person we need to add to that list."

Tension rippled through Clint. Had she recalled something new or was this the thing he'd sensed she was holding back?

"Art Rosen." She moistened her lips and stared at the bottle of beer for a moment. "He and I had a brief affair when I first came on board at the firm. I've never told anyone about it, but… I said I'd be completely truthful." She glanced at Clint. "This is deeply personal and, frankly, I'm ashamed I allowed it to happen."

Clint wanted to reach out and touch her, to let her know he understood, but this wasn't the time. "We all have our uncomfortable secrets."

"Some more than others," Harper said with a pointed look at Clint. He tipped his beer up and had a long swallow.

"I have a secret," Lori said.

Harper's expression fell.

Lori laughed and held up her beer. "Don't worry, I'm not pregnant. I wouldn't be having a beer." She punched her husband on the shoulder.

"Don't get me wrong." Harper held up his hands. "I want more babies. But first we need a bigger house. When Chester is here, it gets pretty tight."

Chester was Chet's son with his first wife. The kid started kindergarten this year. Chet was already certain his son was the next Einstein. The kid was damned smart. That was another thing about his friends, Clint realized. Moments like this, they made him yearn for his own family.

"Cook is planning to pop the question to Addi," Lori said.

Harper made a face. "How do you know this and I don't?"

"Because he showed me the ring he was planning to buy. He wanted a woman's opinion."

"Addi's a catch." Clint was glad the relationship had worked out for the two despite Cook's prior relationship with Dr. Sylvia Baron who also happened to be Addi's biological mother. It wasn't until Addi came to Birmingham in search of her biological mother that Addi and Cook met.

"I'm sorry," Harper spoke up, "but that relationship is going to take some therapy if you ask me."

"It was complicated," Lori explained for Natalie's benefit. "Cook and Addi's mother had a relationship a couple of years ago. They've worked it all out and I'm thrilled for them."

Harper shrugged. "Me, too. Addi's hot."

Lori's jaw dropped and even Natalie laughed at Harper's remark.

"Sylvia's sister Nina is planning the engagement party," Lori warned. "Jess says it will be the event of the year. You'll have to wear a suit."

Harper groaned and the women laughed again.

Clint was grateful for the *normal* chatter. Natalie needed a dose of normalcy. He had a good idea that it had been a long time since she'd felt that way. He hated to be the one who drew her back to the painful reality of the present. "Would you have shared your misgivings about the Thompson case with Rosen?"

Natalie considered the question for a moment. "Our affair ended two years before that case. He was my mentor and friend. Nothing more," she added as if she sensed he needed to understand. "I have no recall of going to him with any concerns."

"But," Clint countered, "he's the one you would have gone to."

She met his gaze, uncertainty in hers. "Yes."

"Art Rosen," Lori said as she wrote the name on the makeshift case board. She drew a line from his name to Farago's and inserted the firm's name between them.

"Beckett is a wild card," Harper said. "We don't know who hired him. Chances are it was Farago. I don't see a senior partner getting his hands that dirty."

"Agreed," Clint said. "We should add any private investigators the firm hired on the case."

"There was only one," Natalie said. "Donald Murray."

"I think he retired," Harper noted.

"As long as he didn't move to some exotic island finding him shouldn't be a problem." Clint wasn't familiar with the man, but he would find him.

"Let me run his name in the morning," Lori offered. "Save you some time."

"I appreciate that." Clint might not admit it out loud, but he missed these brainstorming sessions with the team. He suspected that Jess did, as well.

Layla woke from her nap and demanded her mother's attention while Harper saw them out. When they reached Clint's car, Natalie hesitated before getting in. "Your friends are nice. I can see why you made such a good team."

"We got off to a bumpy start, but we pulled it together." She settled into the passenger seat and Clint closed her door. He rounded the hood to the driver's side. When he'd first been assigned to SPU, he'd been on a mission. Chief of Police Burnett had asked Clint to keep an eye on Jess since the serial killer obsessed with her was still on the loose at the time. It hadn't taken then Chief Jess Harris long to figure out what Clint was up to. Thankfully, the team accepted him anyway.

Lori, Harper and Cook were the first people he'd let this close to him. He intended to keep them close.

Lately he'd been feeling the urge for something he'd sworn he would never want again. He stole a glance at the woman next to him. He knew better than to trust those feelings.

The sooner he wrapped up this investigation, the better for all involved.

11:45 p.m.

THE WHISPERS WOKE HER.

Natalie threw back the covers and sat up, dropping her feet to the cool floor. She closed her eyes and allowed the sounds to envelop her.

No...laughter—April's laughter. *We can't...she might hear us. If David found out…*

She won't tell—the man's deep voice. *I need a drink. Didn't you say the liquor cabinet is in your father's study? Come on...*

Natalie's eyes opened. Her father's study. She used his study as an office. Could she have hidden something there? Was that what the dark whispers were trying to help her remember?

Heart thundering, she hurried to the stairs. For a moment she stood there, recalling that fateful night. She'd come out of her room. Why would she come out of her room at that time of night?

Her body trembling, she grasped the bannister and closed her eyes, trying harder to recall the events. *Relax, let the memories come. No fear. No resistance.*

The sound of secret laughter, so soft it was barely audible swept past her. Her breath caught as if her sister's very presence had just touched her.

Come on, the man whispered. *Nat will kill*

me, April protested. *Shhh...we won't wake her*, the man promised. April and the man had gone downstairs.

Natalie opened her eyes. Her sister's laughter had awakened her that night. Natalie held very still, allowed the memories to surface. She remembered climbing out of bed, dragging on her robe, and padding to the stairs. Then...

She was falling.

This is your fault.

Natalie clung to the bannister, her lungs struggling for air. Who had said those words? *This is your fault.* Male, for sure. Harsh, deep...a growl. The voice was at once familiar and at the same time completely alien. Had a man pushed her? The man with April? Not David, it seemed.

The night of Natalie's fall her sister had claimed she was angry with David, which was the reason she'd decided to come to her childhood home and spend the night. Had April lied just to have a secret rendezvous with her lover? But why would a man Natalie didn't know try to hurt her?

Could April's lover have been Vince? Natalie couldn't see that match under any circumstances.

Where had the secret lover been when the ambulance arrived? Had he taken off, leaving April alone with her gravely injured sister?

"You always did know how to pick them," Natalie muttered.

She steadied herself and descended the stairs. At least she hadn't awakened Clint. She resisted the urge to look in on him. As much as she would love a glimpse of his bare chest, there was something else she had to do right now.

Holding her breath she eased apart the pocket doors of what she would always call her father's study. Though she had years ago packed his files and stored them away, many of the things that made the room his space remained. She turned on the light and went to the liquor cabinet. She opened the doors and surveyed the variety of liquors her father had prided himself on collecting. Most were decades old and unopened. Her father had rarely partaken, but he'd felt the need to have a variety available for guests. She opened a door and touched the rich wood of the humidor that still held his special occasion cigars.

She smiled. Whenever she opened that humidor the scent of fine tobacco made her think of her father. She closed the doors and tension banded around her chest. The air fled her lungs.

The sound of doors and drawers slamming echoed in her ears. She closed her eyes and told herself to relax. She had hurried from her bedroom…saw the intruder at the bottom of the stairs.

She frowned and took a moment to sort the memories. This new one wasn't from the night of her fall, it was from Monday morning when she'd shot an intruder.

Wait. Natalie opened her eyes. The intruder—Beckett, she reminded herself—hadn't been facing the stairs as if he were looking upward. He had been facing the direction of the great room, his back to...

This room. Her father's study. Her office.

Natalie turned around, surveying the room she had loved her whole life. It made her feel close to her father.

The intruder had been *here*...looking for something.

It's in your hands now.

Natalie tried to breathe.

You're the only one who can make it right.

Imogene Stuart's voice whispered through Natalie's mind. Imogene had given her something. A new statement about what happened in that hospital room. Stuart had been in the corridor on the phone. She'd just found out her husband was dying with cancer. She was upset. She couldn't even afford to take a day off to be with him. The treatments were incredibly expensive. Her insurance wouldn't cover everything.

She'd lied to secure her early retirement and for the money Rison Medical offered her. Money she needed for her husband's treatments, but neither the money nor the treatments had saved him. He died anyway. On his deathbed he'd begged her to tell the truth. She had called Natalie. They'd met at the funeral home. She'd given Natalie the amended statement. That was the reason Natalie hadn't remembered any of this when she was at her house today. She and Stuart had met at the funeral home where the poor woman had been picking out her husband's coffin.

Natalie gasped for air.

The evidence was here. *Somewhere*.

If she had to take this room apart she would find it. She started with the desk. She removed drawers, dumping their contents on top of the desk, and then looking on the underside as well as in the cavity. When every single drawer in the room had been emptied, she moved on to the shelves and cabinets.

"What're we looking for?"

Natalie dropped the books she'd moved from the shelf. Her heart launched into her throat. "Good Lord, you scared the hell out of me."

Clint was at her side, retrieving the books before she could get a breath past the band around her chest. She might have helped him with the books if she hadn't gotten lost staring at his naked torso.

"Where do you want these?"

Just watching his muscles bunch and flex as he

reached and grabbed and then straightened made her wish for a long cool drink.

"What?"

"The books?" He held up two handfuls.

"Look through them for any document I might have hidden." *Focus, Natalie.* "Then put them in the stack over by the chair."

She turned back to the bookshelves. *Keep your wits.* This was too important to be thinking about anything else.

As they rifled through book after book, looked on top of and under every item in the room, she explained her most recent memories.

"I don't understand." She braced her hip against the desk and rubbed her temples with her fingertips. The inability to find what she absolutely knew she had possessed was so damned maddening. "It has to be here."

He turned the leather executive chair upside down as if it weighed nothing at all and made sure nothing was taped on the under side. "At least now you know you had evidence."

"If I can get Mrs. Stuart to talk, I won't need the evidence. Her husband urged her to tell the truth. I can use his final wish as leverage."

Clint placed the chair back on its wheels. "It's been two years. His dying wish may not carry as much weight now." He threaded the fingers of one hand through his hair.

Natalie so needed something to relieve her dry throat. "True. I guess when I failed to follow through she decided to put it all behind her. Now her life is about self-preservation. I can understand that."

He came around to her side of the desk. "You should go back to bed."

This close, his scent enveloped her, made her want to lean into him. Memories of the way he'd kissed her had her knees growing weak.

"Don't look at me that way, Natalie."

"I don't know what you mean," she lied.

"You're just getting your life back and you still have a long way to go. You don't need a man like me."

She dared to touch him, the slightest brush of her fingertips across his contoured chest. His skin felt hot and so smooth. "What kind of man are you?"

Those dark brown eyes blackened. "A man with a not-so-appealing history that too often comes back to haunt him."

"That part of your past is irrelevant to me." Her heart pounding, she reached up and touched his lean jaw, trailed her fingers along the sharp angle and traced the softer, fuller ridge of his lips. She trembled while he stood stone still. "You aren't attracted to me? Your kiss said differently."

He curled his fingers around her wrist and

pulled her hand away from his face. "The kiss was a mistake. A lapse in judgment. You hired me to help you solve this case. Have you changed your mind? Maybe you've decided you want to hire the man I used to be."

She watched his lips move as he spoke and she wanted to feel them against hers again more than she wanted to draw in her next breath.

He backed her against the desk and pressed her down onto the cluttered surface, his face not an inch from hers, his body crushed intimately against hers. "Are you sure this is what you want?" He brushed his lips across hers. "I can pleasure you like no one else ever has." He tasted her mouth again. "I can touch you so intimately you won't ever think of sex the same way. Is that what you want?"

She couldn't speak…she whimpered.

"Tell me that's what you want. That you want me to do this now. Here. And I'll do it."

Anger flared in his eyes.

He didn't want this.

He didn't want her.

She flattened her hands against his chest. "Get off me."

"I thought this was what you wanted," he growled.

"No."

He moved off her so fast, she lost her balance just lifting herself up.

He stood at the window staring out into the darkness. His arms folded over his chest. The rigid set of his shoulders told her he was furious.

Part of her wanted to apologize but the other part, the needy woman inside, wanted to demand why he didn't want her. She'd thought he did when he kissed her that once.

She chose the coward's way out. "Good night."

He said nothing as she left the room.

Tomorrow morning she was going back to see Imogene Stuart. And then she was getting justice for the Thompson family.

Chapter Thirteen

Southwood Road
Saturday, September 24, 8:30 a.m.

Clint poured the remainder of his second cup of coffee down the drain. He rinsed the cup and set it on the counter. He should apologize for his behavior last night. Natalie was not speaking to him this morning. She'd taken her coffee into her home office and closed the doors.

He'd walked past the door half a dozen times. From the sounds on the other side she was either still searching for the evidence Stuart had given her or she was attempting to organize the mess she'd made last night. He should offer to help.

No. He plowed his fingers through his hair. Spending too much time in a confined space with her was a bad idea. He braced his hands on the sink and stared out the window. His freshman year in college he'd learned to disengage emo-

tionally with the blink of an eye. The call came
and he stepped into character. It was that simple.
In the beginning the need to disengage was about
survival. He turned off his emotions and turned
on the charm along with his physical prowess.
He'd done his research, learned how to give what
his client wanted even if the client didn't know
how to articulate the desire. The human body
had all sorts of pleasure points. He learned how
to manipulate each one.

He hadn't gone looking for the work that had
changed his life. Supply and demand—that had
been the name of the game. He hadn't been naive.
He'd recognized his looks were his most readily
marketable asset. So he wrangled a fake driver's
license that said he was twenty-one and hit the
classier bars in hopes of landing a bartender position. He knew how to work a crowd and he was
banking on good tips keeping his rent paid.

Regrettably for him, that year it seemed every
damned body wanted to tend bar. After the tenth
rejection he'd basically given up. An older man,
probably Clint's age now, had stopped him as he
left the last ill-fated interview. Clint remembered
being impressed with his suit and the Rolex he
wore. The man had explained how Clint could
earn all the money he would ever need. Women
with only money to keep them company would
gladly take care of him for a little attention. Of

course he'd resisted the idea at first. When an eviction notice landed on his apartment door, he did what he had to do.

He refused to regret his decision or the time he'd spent giving his clients pleasure whether it was nothing more than an escort to a dinner party or it was a no-holds-barred all-nighter.

In all these years since he'd left that part of his life behind, he hadn't been able to teach himself to engage emotionally. Relationships never lasted. Until he'd joined the SPU he'd even avoided maintaining friendships. He had spent his entire adult life dodging emotional entanglements. Period. The problem was the past two years working with Jess and the team had undone most of his hardearned indifference and desire for solitude.

He watched the people he considered friends form permanent bonds and have children and suddenly he felt the building need to have those things, as well. It was the proverbial want what you can't have syndrome. Or, in his case, it was what he didn't know how to have.

"I'd like to apologize."

Clint turned around, surprised that Natalie had managed to get as close as the kitchen doorway without him sensing her approach. "Apologize for what?"

Her shoulders stiffened ever so slightly. He liked the soft blue sweater she wore. It matched her eyes. The jeans did a stellar job of reminding him of all those lush curves he'd felt beneath him last night. Desire stirred at the memory. *Very bad move.*

She brought her cup to the sink. He stepped aside. She rinsed the cup as he had and placed it on the counter. "I've allowed the stress and uncertainty to cloud my judgment. I haven't been thinking clearly." She met his gaze. "Rest assured it will not happen again. I'd like to pay another visit to Imogene Stuart. Since I can't find the evidence she gave me, perhaps I can convince her to cooperate."

He was supposed to be happy to hear this news. She'd just taken full responsibility for his misstep. Instead, he wanted to kiss her until she admitted she wanted him as desperately right now as she clearly had last night. The concept that touching her or kissing her might not happen again was unacceptable, yet she was right. It could not happen again.

His cell vibrated, preventing him from repeating last night's stupidity. He answered without checking the screen, which would have required he take his eyes off hers and for some ridiculous reason he couldn't do that. "Hayes."

"It's Lori. Imogene Stuart is dead."

Clint looked away from the concern gathering in Natalie's eyes. He didn't want her to see the defeat in his own. This was a major setback. Potentially, Stuart was the only person who could confirm what Natalie remembered about the Thompson case. "What happened?"

"Her daughter came to pick her up for a weekend trip they had planned. When she didn't answer the door she went inside and found her still in bed. She thought she'd had a heart attack or maybe a stroke, but the ME says she was suffocated. We think the perp used her pillow. Sometime between midnight and three this morning."

Damn. "Was anything taken from the house?"

"There's no indication of forced entry. Nothing out of place. The daughter doesn't believe anything is missing, but she's pretty upset."

Clint blew out a disgusted breath. "They took the only thing that mattered." Stuart was dead, her life stolen. The truth snatched again from the Thompson family. Natalie would be left with regret for putting her in the line of fire with yesterday's visit. She would shoulder the responsibility for the woman's murder. "Let me know if you find anything or if the family knows anything at all about our case."

"Will do," Lori assured him.

Clint thanked her and ended the call. "That was Lori. Imogene Stuart is dead."

"Was she…?"

He nodded.

Natalie pressed her hand over her mouth. Tears brimmed on her lashes.

"There doesn't appear to be anything missing in her home. If she kept a copy of the evidence she gave you, it could be hidden there somewhere or in a bank deposit box. Lori will give us a hand on that end by searching thoroughly and questioning the family. At this point, that's about all we can do."

Natalie hugged her arms around her chest. "I want to talk to April, in person, and then I intend to talk to Vince."

She was distraught and definitely not thinking clearly. "Do you think it's a good idea to tip our hand since there's a good chance Farago is involved on some level?" Natalie's safety was Clint's primary concern. As badly as he wanted to nail these bastards, he would not sacrifice her security.

"I intend to finish this before anyone else dies."

When she would have walked out, he stopped her with a hand on her arm. The contact was like grabbing a live wire. The heat and energy rushed through his body. "It's my job to finish this," he reminded her, "but more important it's my job to protect you."

"Don't worry." She drew away from his touch. "I'm well aware of what you're here to do."

He supposed it was better for her to be angry

with him than to keep testing the boundaries he struggled to maintain. His focus could not be divided—as tempting as taking what she'd offered was. The brain injury she'd suffered made her even more vulnerable. As foolish as the idea was, he didn't want her to want him only to get through this hard time in her life. It was an irrational idea, but as hard as he worked not to be, he was only human.

Before entering the garage, he scanned for signs of entry during the night and then he checked his car for any indication of tampering. He'd learned the ways to protect himself from that kind of surprise. Alarm systems could be bypassed but there were other measures. Like the tape he'd put in strategic locations around the hood as well as the doors. He checked for loss of fluids and damage to the tires.

When he felt confident there were no surprises, he opened the passenger door for her and then climbed behind the wheel. She was focused inward, likely beating herself up for yesterday's visit to Stuart.

He backed out of the garage. When the overhead door had closed, he rolled out onto the street and drove in the direction of her sister's house. "This isn't your fault, Natalie."

"It is my fault. You mentioned that someone might be watching us and I disregarded that warning."

He glanced at her, wished he could touch her. Damn him, last night had been the straw that broke the camel's back. Beyond that one kiss, he'd managed fairly well to restrain his desire for her—his need to touch her—and then he'd gone stupid and tried to scare her off. All he'd actually done was push himself over the edge he'd been avoiding for years.

"The people responsible for this want you to feel that way. Don't give them the satisfaction, Natalie. They did this. You tried to stop them once and they almost killed you. Now you're back, fighting for justice again."

She shook her head. "If we can't find proof of what really happened in the Thompson case, they'll get away with it. Mrs. Stuart will have died for nothing. If my brain would work right… maybe…"

He spared her a glance, the worry in her eyes making his gut clench. "We won't let that happen."

She stared straight ahead. "You're right. We have to find the truth. The Thompson family and the Stuart family deserve justice and I want my life back."

He wished he could promise her the kind of outcome she and those families deserved. Unfortunately, even if they found the evidence she needed, he suspected some things would never be the same again. Too many of the people she cared about were involved and the TBI would always have an impact on her life.

There were some things that couldn't be undone. They would know soon enough if her sister had played a part that couldn't be taken back. Certainly Vince Farago had. His actions may have been with the full knowledge of Rosen. How often did such a big case get turned around at the last moment without the involvement of the upper echelon of the hierarchy?

Never.

18th Avenue South, Five Points
10:20 a.m.

NATALIE STARED AT her cell. "April never goes anywhere without her cell. I don't understand why she hasn't called me back or at least responded to my text."

"Maybe she's at the spa." Clint hoped her sister was just out spending her husband's money. "You sure about this?" He glanced at the craftsman-style cottage that sat on a postage-stamp-size lot in one of the city's most highly sought after neighborhoods. Vince Farago had good taste if nothing else. Bastard.

Natalie followed his gaze. "I'm sure. I'm only a couple of years late."

Clint wasn't so certain. A confrontation with Farago or maybe even Natalie's trust in him likely had set the events of two years ago in motion. Someone at the firm had learned what she was doing and taken steps to stop her. Whatever Farago or one of his cronies had done then, he wouldn't have the opportunity to do it this time.

They exited the car and walked up the cobblestone path leading to the sprawling front porch that was larger than the front lawn. Farago wasn't married but that didn't mean he didn't have a companion inside. Proceeding with caution was necessary. Until this was over, the last thing they needed was word to get out that Natalie Drummond was delving into the Thompson-Rison Medical case. There were far too many legal issues that might put a stop to their investigation.

Clint rang the bell and waited. Farago showed up at the door wearing jeans and nothing else. He stared at them for a moment before opening the door as if he understood he wasn't going to like the purpose of their visit and certainly didn't want the neighbors overhearing.

"What an unexpected surprise," Farago said, his tone as well as his posture suggesting their visit was no surprise at all. "I was just about to have coffee," he went on. "Come in. Join me." He glanced at Clint, but his gaze lingered on Natalie the longest.

Clint wondered if the two had shared more than a working relationship. Not that he could blame Farago. Natalie was a beautiful, smart, sophisticated woman. She deserved a hell of a lot better than either of the two men staring at her just now.

"We need to talk," Natalie told him, her voice cold.

Farago ignored her icy tone and closed the door behind them. Beyond the entry hall, the living space had been opened up into one large room that looked out over downtown Birmingham.

"Nice view," Clint commented.

"I hear yours is better." Farago picked up a glass and downed the orange juice.

"I wasn't aware you kept up with my real estate ventures."

"Only the ones that involve the most valuable residential real estate downtown." He set the glass aside and reached for a mug. "You're sure you won't have coffee?"

"No thank you," Natalie said with a firm shake of her head.

When Farago looked to Clint, Clint shook his head, as well.

"So." Farago filled his cup. "What do the two of you want to discuss this morning? Frankly,

I'm surprised to see you after the unpleasant exchange we had yesterday." He looked from one to the other. "Don't be shy, have a seat." He gestured to the stools flanking the island.

Ignoring his invitation, Natalie demanded, "Tell me why you ignored the truth in the Thompson-Rison Medical case?"

Farago looked at her for a long moment then shrugged. "What truth are you referring to? We all have our own versions of the truth, after all."

"The day before I ended up in the hospital fighting for my life, I learned the only truth that mattered in the case." She moved closer to the island. "But I think you already knew that."

He grabbed a piece of browned bread from the toaster and tore off a bite. "I have no idea what you're talking about," he said between chews.

"Imogene Stuart told me everything." Natalie shook her head. "She told me all about the cover-up. Even gave me the evidence I needed to prove it. But then I took that untimely dive down the stairs."

Farago tossed the bread onto the counter. "What cover-up are you talking about?" He shot Clint a glance. "Has she had her meds this morning?"

Clint faked a smile. "You have no idea how badly I want to hurt you, Farago, so I would suggest that you watch your mouth."

Farago rolled his eyes. "Cut to the chase, Nat. What evidence?"

"Stuart left Mr. Thompson unattended and he fell. The resulting head injury that went ignored for hours cost him his life."

A real smile tilted Clint's lips as he watched Natalie in action. One of these days, when she was fully recovered, he wanted to watch her in the courtroom.

Another of those indifferent shrugs lifted Farago's arrogant shoulders. "If that's true, why didn't Stuart say so two years ago?"

"Because she was paid to keep quiet. Are you the one who took the offer to her?"

He held up his hands. "I have no idea what you're talking about. You do realize that what you're doing is—"

"I know exactly what I'm doing," Natalie assured him. "I'm fully aware of the ramifications for a number of people, including me. I would have done this two years ago except someone stopped me. So I'm doing it now," she warned.

Farago continued to appear unfazed. "Then why don't you and Stuart take this theory you have to a judge. Why beat around the bush?"

"Stuart is dead," Clint informed him. "She was murdered in her home last night. Where were you this morning between midnight and three?"

"I was with friends at the Rare Martini over on Seventh until midnight. Then I came home. Alone."

"So you don't have an alibi." Clint wasn't sure Farago had the guts to kill anyone, but that didn't mean he wasn't responsible for the woman's death. If Rosen told him to get it done, Farago would have found a way.

"I'm afraid not and you don't have a badge." He turned his attention back to Natalie. "Really, Nat, you and your sidekick need to practice your good cop–bad cop routine. I'm not unsettled in the least."

"I'm happy for you, Vince," Natalie said, her voice empty. "Because I feel responsible for her death. If I hadn't gone to see her yesterday, she would still be alive. She's dead because of my actions."

"I guess that's one you'll have to live with, huh?" Farago sipped his coffee. "Life is hard that way sometimes."

Natalie smiled. "Oh, wait, there's one other thing, I failed to mention. I have the evidence, Vince."

Farago's posture changed so subtly Clint would have missed it had he not been watching him so closely. Natalie had hit a nerve. Clint wanted to tell her to slow it down, but he had a feeling her intention was to bait Farago. Bad idea. Farago would go straight to Rosen.

"Like I said," Vince tossed back, "take it to a judge."

Natalie laughed. "You think I'm bluffing."

Farago flattened his hands on the marble counter top. "I *know* you're bluffing."

And there it was. Fury charged through Clint. He wanted to beat the hell out of the guy. The bastard was somehow involved in what had happened to Natalie, there was no denying it. He couldn't possibly know the evidence was missing unless he'd been a party to taking it.

"I thought you might," Natalie said. "Thank you, Vince. That's all I needed to know."

His face paled as he realized his faux pas. "Wait a minute, I—"

"Goodbye, Vince." Natalie turned and headed for the door.

Clint gave his old nemesis a nod and followed the same route.

"Natalie, wait!" Farago rushed to catch up with them. "You really need to think about this. You're throwing away your career. What firm is going to want you after this?"

She stopped at the door and glared at him. "I think that's already been done for me, wouldn't you say?"

"You don't know what they're capable of," Farago warned.

"Who?" Natalie demanded. "*You* and who else?"

"It's Rosen," Farago said quickly when Natalie reached for the door once more. "He'll do anything to stay on top. *Anything*. If that woman is dead, he'll be the one who ordered it."

"Are you willing to help stop him?" Clint asked. "I'm confident a plea deal could be reached if you were involved in Beckett's or Stuart's murder. Maybe even immunity."

Farago shook his head. "You don't understand. None of us will live long enough to care."

Chapter Fourteen

11:10 a.m.

"Did your sister say what she wanted to talk about?"

Natalie forced her fingers to relax before they cracked her cell phone. No sooner than they'd left Vince, April had returned Natalie's call. She was waiting for Natalie at the house. "She didn't tell me. She only said that it was urgent."

Clint drove a little faster. Natalie's heart seemed intent to do the same. Vince's words were still ringing in her ears. How could she have worked at the firm all those years and not understood what Rosen and Vince were capable of? She was no neophyte. She was well aware of the ways of the world. Her law school professors had made it clear the kinds of evil their students would encounter in their future careers. Maybe she'd still worn the rose-colored glasses just the same. She had considered herself and Vince part of the good guys. Rosen had been her mentor. She'd thought he was the perfect example of an upstanding attorney.

She had been wrong.

April's Mercedes waited in the driveway as Clint made the turn. He tapped the garage door opener they'd taken from Natalie's crashed car and waited for the door to lift, and then he rolled into the space where her BMW usually sat. At some point she needed to get a new car. She wasn't sure she would ever feel safe again in the old one. For now, she felt safest with Clint.

Don't do this, Natalie.

Her last relationship had ended nearly two years ago. She hadn't really had time to feel alone considering her entire focus had been on recovery. April had been at her side. Suzanna and Leonard had been with her every day after she came home.

Now the sting of loneliness burned deep. She was thirty-two years old, almost thirty-three, and she had no one except her sister and brother. Suzanna and Leonard had quit. Her colleagues wanted nothing else to do with her—the feeling was mutual. Clint turned off the engine and closed the overhead door.

The two of them were very similar except he had more friends. She suspected Clint's single status was by choice. Had his early career ruined him for relationships? She imagined many of the women he had…attended to…had husbands who ignored them. Natalie's only excuse was that she had always been too focused on work.

And just look where that has gotten you, Nat.

"There's something you want to ask?"

His question startled her. She hadn't realized she was staring at him. "Sorry. I was just thinking."

"About?"

"It's nothing." She reached for the door. "April's waiting."

Clint stopped her with a hand on her arm. Her body reacted instantly to his touch, aching for far more. She dared to meet his eyes.

"You are an amazing woman, Natalie. You don't need the firm or anyone else. Once this is over, put it all behind you and embrace the life you deserve with someone who deserves you."

He let her go and emerged from the car. Natalie drew in a shaky breath and steadied herself. When this was done, she and Clint were going to have a long talk. He didn't give himself enough credit.

April stood in the middle of the great room. Her face was red from crying. She glanced at Clint. "We have to talk privately, Nat."

Natalie sat down on the sofa. "Whatever you

have to say, you can say it in front of Clint. He's here to help us."

April collapsed into the closest chair. "Us?"

Clint drifted to the other side of the room, giving them space. Natalie appreciated his effort to make April more comfortable. She nodded in answer to her sister's question. "He'll help us figure out whatever has to be done."

A frown furrowed April's brow. "I don't think you understand."

"You were here the night I fell down the stairs. You said you and David had a fight."

April's eyes widened slightly. "We did."

"You had a man here with you," Natalie went on, "someone with whom you were having an affair."

Her sister's face paled. "I didn't think you remembered."

"I wasn't completely sure the details were accurate until you confirmed them just now." She drew in a deep breath. "You were laughing. I woke up. When I realized you were in your old room with someone who wasn't David, I decided to go downstairs for coffee and to think."

April's face crumpled. Tears flowed down her cheeks. "I'm so sorry. I'm the reason you fell. If I hadn't gotten involved with that bastard, you… Oh my God." She buried her face in her hands.

Natalie held her emotions in check. She had to

know everything before she allowed herself to feel. Whatever April had done or had allowed to happen, the truth had to come out. There was no more time for games, too many people had suffered already. "Did you or your friend leave your room before you heard me scream?"

Scrubbing at her tears, April's frown deepened. "What? No. We heard you scream. I jumped up and pulled on my gown. He was still dragging on his jeans when I ran out of the room." Realization dawned and her expression turned guarded. "Why do you ask?"

"Someone may have pushed me, April."

"You think I did that?" She shot to her feet, her arms going instinctively around her thin body. "I can't believe you would think that. We're sisters, Nat. I would never hurt you."

"What about your friend?" Natalie refused to look away even when her sister's trembling tore at her heart.

"I told you he was still in the room when I ran out. You were at the bottom of the stairs when I found you. He couldn't have pushed you." She dropped back into her chair. "Oh my God. This just gets worse."

"Then someone else was in the house."

April shook her head. "I never saw anyone else. The jerk took off while I was calling 9-1-1. There was no one else, Natalie. I swear. It was just the three of us until he took off and help arrived."

For a moment Natalie started to doubt her theory. Had she tripped, rather than been pushed? Was the feeling in that one memory one that had been planted by all the deceit she had uncovered?

"I know he didn't push you," April said, drawing Natalie back to the present, "but he was the one who tampered with your air bag."

"How do you know this?" Clint came up behind Natalie. He braced his hands on the sofa.

April swiped her eyes. "When you told the police the intruder had a scar, I knew it was him." She touched her forehead between her eyebrows. "I couldn't believe it. Other people could have scars there, too, but then I remembered the stuff he told me."

"What stuff?" Clint pressed.

Natalie was glad Clint asked. Her mouth felt full of cotton, her chest so tight she couldn't possibly hope to breathe.

"He worked for the dealership." She dropped her gaze to the floor. "The one where you bought your car. Before your accident, David was looking at BMWs and this man who worked there was looking at me. He was everything David wasn't. Drop dead gorgeous with lots of muscle. I was desperate for attention so we started seeing each other." She pressed her fingers to her lips before going on. "At first it was just great sex, then he started telling me stories about how easy it was to cause brake failure and all sorts of other problems. He bragged about how he could control the people who hired him to do that kind of work. He said that once some low-level dirtbag hired him to do something to a brake line. Then when the guy didn't pay up, he repaired it before the owner of the car even had a clue what had happened. He laughed and said people turned over their key rings when they had their cars serviced. The dealership has one of those machines that make copies of keys. He went on and on about how security systems are jokes."

Natalie exchanged a look with Clint.

"His name," Natalie said, her voice taut, "was Mike Beckett."

April gasped. "How did you know?"

"The police lab found evidence of her brakes having been tampered with previously and then repaired," Clint explained. "It wasn't difficult to trace the activity back to the dealership."

"He did that to you?" April's face darkened to a deep shade of furious red. "I swear I didn't know. Bastard."

"Were you still involved with him after my injury?" Natalie felt numb now. Beckett had used April to get to her. Now the most important step was determining who hired him.

April shook her head. "Not after that night." Her watery gaze settled on Natalie. "After you were hurt. I never even thought of him again until you crashed your car. It was easy to put together the intruder with the air bag tampering." Her voice sounded so hollow, her gaze distant. "The scar was too much of a coincidence considering what he had told me before."

Suddenly Natalie understood. The bottom dropped from her stomach. "What did you do, April?"

April glanced at Clint briefly and then settled her gaze on Natalie. "I went to his house and demanded to know if he was the one who broke into your house and messed with your car."

She fell silent for a long moment before she continued. "He said he didn't have to break in. He'd made a copy of your key the last time you had your car serviced. I slapped him and he tried to push me away. He said he would have killed you when you caught him in your house, but you shot him first."

Silence lapsed again while Natalie's heart continued to break.

"Then he told me to leave. He said if I told anyone they would kill you and Heath. I tried my best to get him to tell me who paid him to do this and he wouldn't say."

"April," Natalie began but her sister held up a hand to stop her.

"That's when I saw the gun."

Natalie's heart surged into her throat. "April, don't say anything else."

Her sister shook her head, tears flowing down her cheeks. "I killed him."

Natalie's hand went to her mouth to hold back a sob.

"I grabbed the gun and pointed it at him. I told him he'd better stay away from my family and he just laughed." She shrugged. "He said he would put a bullet in my head and make it look as if you shot me. He tried to take the gun from me and somehow during the struggle it went off."

"You came here and changed," Clint suggested.

April nodded. "I was in your closet getting something to put on when Suzanna came into the room. I hid the clothes and the gun in a trash bag in your clothes hamper so Suzanna wouldn't see."

"You came back for...them." Natalie was so relieved that she hadn't imagined the whole thing that she felt lightheaded.

"Yes. I put them in a trash bin downtown."

"Where exactly?" Clint demanded.

April looked taken aback.

"It's all right," Natalie assured her. "It was self-defense. Beckett threatened you. But we have to let the police know what happened."

"Oh God. David doesn't know. If he finds out… I'm so sorry, Nat. I wasn't thinking of anything except how it was my fault. I had to try and make him stop."

Natalie refused to let her emotions get the better of her. "David is a smart man. He'll forgive you and stand by you if he wants to be governor one day." Maybe if he hadn't been so interested in running for office he wouldn't have left April vulnerable to an affair. Perhaps that was a stretch but blood was thicker than water. "I know you were trying to help and that means a great deal to me, but a man is dead and we have to do this by the book."

April reluctantly gave Clint the address and he called his friends in the BPD.

Natalie and April hugged. Her sister had been there for Natalie through her darkest days; Natalie had to be here for her now. They needed each other.

One thing nagged at her though. Suzanna had known April was in Natalie's closet. What else did Suzanna know that she hadn't told Natalie?

3:15 p.m.

NATALIE SAT ON the sofa on one side of April and her husband, David, sat on the other while Lieutenant Harper took her statement. Detective Cook had recovered the trash bag from the trash bin and called the BPD's evidence collection team.

"Will she be arrested?" David asked, his somber tone uncharacteristically quiet.

"Not at this time, sir," Harper explained. "When we sort this all out, we'll see how it stacks up. For now, it certainly sounds as if Mrs. Keating felt her life was in danger and acted in self-defense."

"I hope we can keep this out of the media," David urged.

"I can't promise that." Harper put his notepad and handheld recorder away. "But the department has no reason to talk to the media regarding the details we've just learned." He stood. "I have everything I need for now."

"Thank you, Lieutenant." Natalie was grateful Clint's friends in SPU had the case considering it was now a homicide investigation. She felt confident Harper would do all he could to protect April.

Clint showed the detective to the door.

David stood and held out his hand to his wife. "I think we should go home now." He smiled at Natalie, but the expression fell short of his eyes. "I'm certain you're exhausted. This has been a harrowing week for you."

Natalie rose. "I love my sister, David. I hope you're not holding back on my account. She's suffered enough over this. I would hate to hear that you caused her any additional distress."

He nodded his understanding as he drew April into the shelter of his arms. "You're a good sister, Natalie, even after you've been through so much yourself. You have my word that April and I are fine. She's the love of my life. We've both made mistakes. It's where we go from here that matters."

Though her brother-in-law's speech sounded less than passionate, Natalie nodded. "We'll all get through this."

Clint had just closed the front door as they moved into the entry hall.

"Until we know," he said to David, "who hired Beckett to hurt your family, I would advise you to keep April close. Watch each other's backs."

"With the election coming up next year, competition is heating up," David explained. "I've already contacted a security service about around-the-clock protection for both of us." David looked from Clint to Natalie. "I can have my contact there meet with you if you're interested in hiring someone, Nat." He glanced at Clint. "It might not be a bad idea moving forward."

"Thank you, David. I'll let you know." Natalie and April shared another hug before the couple left.

"Well, that went better than I expected," Clint said, echoing her thoughts.

Natalie watched through the leaded glass of the front door as her brother-in-law opened the car door for her sister. "David is a politician through and through. If it's best for his campaign, then he's on board. I just wish I knew what was in his heart."

"I take it you and your brother-in-law aren't the best of friends."

Natalie thought about the question for a moment. "We've never had any real disagreements beyond our differences on political issues. I suppose I always felt that he married April because she was a Drummond. I've never felt close to him, but he has reached out repeatedly since my fall."

Clint's gaze narrowed. "So you felt he wasn't good enough for your sister? He didn't meet the financial criteria or was it something else that made you feel that way?"

The question surprised her. "It wasn't about the money or that he wasn't *good* enough. The Keating family is quite well to do. They moved here about twenty years ago. He and I went to high school together. What I meant about the Drummond name was his impression that the Drummonds were among the founders of the city. I believe that was important to his political aspirations, but it's possible I'm wrong."

Clint looked away. "We should talk to Mr. and Mrs. Clark."

Confused by his odd question, Natalie took a moment to weigh his recommendation. She didn't want to believe that Suzanna might be hiding something from her, but her abrupt departure suggested otherwise.

"If you're up to it," he amended, obviously taking her hesitation for something else.

Natalie squared her shoulders. "Of course." She smoothed the hem of her sweater. "I'm ready."

Two people were dead…because of her. She couldn't think of resting until she found the truth.

Chapter Fifteen

Crestwood Circle
Birmingham
5:45 p.m.

Clint knocked on the door a second time just in case the doorbell wasn't working. Natalie surveyed the yard. She looked nervous. Considering what she'd remembered last night and what she learned from her sister this morning, apprehension was understandable.

Her life had been twisted into a few dozen knots the past couple of years. She deserved a break. He wanted to help her get her life back. He wanted it badly. Maybe more than he'd wanted anything in a long time. He was still kicking himself for questioning her thoughts on David Keating. His feelings of inferiority had nothing to do with her and he had no right dragging her into it.

The door opened and Suzanna Clark schooled

her startled expression as she looked from Natalie to Clint and back. "I've said all I have to say."

Clint had a feeling pressure tactics wouldn't work with the older woman. Not even he would give a lady who reminded him far too much of his mother a hard time. Still, the situation was urgent. Time was not an available luxury at the moment. "Mrs. Clark, I feel compelled to warn you that if you don't cooperate with us, the police will be knocking on your door."

Her face paled. "Leonard!"

Clint winced at the fear he heard in Mrs. Clark's voice.

Natalie reached out to the woman she had known most of her life. "Suzanna, please. I need your help. Please, help me."

"What're you doing here?" Leonard demanded as he bellied up to the door.

"I just want the truth," Natalie pleaded. "I'm certain the two of you have done nothing wrong. This is—"

"Just stop." Suzanna put a hand to her chest. "Come inside."

Leonard sent her a look that spoke loudly of his disapproval.

"Let's just get this over with," Suzanna argued, defeat in her voice. "The police can help them sort it out but we're not helping anyone by remaining silent."

Clint never understood anyone's desire to keep secrets as a means to protect the innocent. The innocent did just fine when secrets were revealed. It was the guilty who didn't fare so well.

Leonard stepped back and Suzanna led them into their home. The brick rancher had a larger than expected living room. Clint sat next to Natalie. Leonard settled into his well-worn recliner next to the matching one his wife chose. He made no bones about how unhappy he was they had appeared at his door. He'd washed his hands of the situation and wanted nothing more to do with Natalie's troubles.

After a lengthy and somewhat awkward silence, Suzanna spoke. "It started a few months before your accident."

Leonard shook his head. "Your folks raised you girls better, but somehow it didn't take as well with April as it did with you."

"April told me about the affair," Natalie spoke up. "The man she was seeing lured her into the relationship. He's the same man who came into my house and tampered with my car."

The couple exchanged another one of those looks. "We," Suzanna said, "suspected he was not a nice man."

Clint was as surprised by the statement as Natalie appeared to be.

"You met him?" Natalie asked.

Suzanna nodded. "She brought him to the house four—"

"Five." Leonard held up one hand, fingers spread wide. "Five times."

"Five," Suzanna amended. "While you were at work. April said they were working on a surprise for you."

"For me?" Natalie shook her head. "What sort of surprise?"

Leonard harrumphed. "The first couple of times they *worked* in your daddy's study. Then they moved their *work* upstairs."

Damn. Clint had hoped April was as innocent in all this as she claimed. "This work," he asked, "was it something more than sex?"

Suzanna's cheeks flamed. Leonard's jaws puffed. "I don't believe so," Suzanna said. "I never found any evidence of anything else."

Leonard shook his head. "The girl should have known she would get caught."

"Wait," Natalie leaned forward a bit, "did you say she got caught? By David?"

"Well," Suzanna hedged, "I can't say that they had any kind of confrontation, but there—"

"He had to know," Leonard protested.

"Why do you think so?" Clint asked. "Was Keating watching the house?"

"He was doing more than that," Leonard said.

"He brought some fellow to the house with him. A security technician or so he said. Claimed there was something wrong with the security system."

"That's preposterous," Natalie argued.

"I'm just telling you what he said. I knew he wasn't exactly telling it like it was because the technician only worked in the entry hall and upstairs."

"In April's old bedroom," Suzanna put in. "I was changing the sheets in your room when they went in there."

"So David suspected." Natalie clasped her hands in her lap. "What else did he do that I don't know about?"

The edge of frustration in her voice told all present that she was not happy to learn there had been so many goings and comings in her home without her knowledge. Clint could see how the Clarks didn't feel comfortable reporting April's activities since she, too, was a Drummond and had grown up in the house. Natalie had likely never given them reason to believe she didn't want her sister on the premises when she wasn't home.

"As far as I know," Suzanna said, "David wasn't in the house again until you came home from the hospital."

"There was that one time," Leonard reminded his wife. "He said he had to get clothes for Natalie."

"I was at the hospital," Suzanna said. "You were in bad shape."

Natalie blinked a couple of times but not before Clint saw the shine of emotion there. Reliving those days was hard enough on her, but to hear that her own family was somehow using her added insult to injury.

"He went upstairs and then he piddled around in the entry hall." Leonard reached for the sweating glass of iced tea on the table next to his chair. "I imagine he was taking out the cameras and such he'd had his *technician* install."

"April came through, though," Suzanna offered. "She and David have tried their best to help since you were hurt. I was hoping everything would be all right now."

Leonard nodded. "He called me or came by every week or two to see if there was anything I needed. Being a husband, I figured he had a right to know what his wife was doing so I put the whole business behind me and tried not to hold his behavior against him. A Christian should never hold bad thoughts against another."

"Me, too." Suzanna looked to her husband. "Until I found the bloody clothes and the gun."

"When Suzanna told me," Leonard said, "I told her we were done. We couldn't be involved with the likes of that. It was bad enough Suzanna could have been there alone when that intruder broke in." Leonard nodded toward Natalie. "I knew you were telling the truth no matter what the police thought. You've never lied or made up nonsense in your life."

Clint resisted the urge to take Natalie's hand in his. She listened patiently but he could feel her tension mounting.

"We're getting older," Suzanna said gently. "It was just too much."

"April said you were there the day she left the gun and the bloody clothes," Natalie ventured.

"We'd been to the grocery store. Leonard always drives me," Suzanna explained. "When we came back her car was in the drive and she was in your shower. I knew she was the one."

"I didn't even want to know what she'd gotten herself into," Leonard admitted. "It was best that we just walked away."

"I wanted to tell you all of it," Suzanna said, "but Leonard didn't want me to get in the middle of it."

"I understand," Natalie assured her. "Please know that you're welcome to come back and I guarantee none of this will happen again. April and her husband have spoken to the police about what happened with the gun and the bloody clothes. There will be an investigation but it has nothing to do with either of you. She and David are standing together on this. He, as you know, is focused on winning this election as a stepping stone to bigger things. He's not going to risk that goal with a nasty divorce."

The couple seemed to consider her offer for a moment. "It's time we retired," Suzanna confessed. "We need to spend more time with our grandchildren."

"I can't blame you." Natalie stood. "Thank you for telling me. If you think of anything else, please don't hesitate to let me know. When I spoke to the police, I didn't mention your names in relation to the gun or the bloody clothes. They have no idea you saw it," she said to Suzanna. "They won't bother you."

Clint had to give her credit, Natalie held it together exceptionally well until they were out of the house and in his car. Even then he wouldn't have known how very upset she was if not for the tears sliding down her cheeks.

"We're taking the evening off," he said. "You need a break."

"What I need is a plane ticket to take me far away from here."

"I'll see what I can do."

He hoped that was a promise he could keep.

Athens-Flatts Building, 2nd Avenue
8:30 p.m.

NATALIE STOOD IN the darkness and watched the lights of downtown Birmingham twinkle. She did love this view from Clint's penthouse. She'd come out onto the grand terrace to feel the cool breeze and to inhale the night air. Her senses came alive just standing here, soaking in the atmosphere. Maybe it was time she sold the house and moved into something more manageable.

Would her parents have wanted her to keep the house if they'd known how much heartache she would suffer there? But then her parents had left her the home because, of their three children, they had known she would be the least likely to sell it or allow it to fall into disrepair. She thought of all the happy years the family had shared in the home. Endless Christmases and birthdays. So many happy memories…and a few devastating ones, as well.

She was not in a good place for making that kind of decision. The aches she felt went deep. Her sister had used Natalie's home and her trust. Her brother-in-law had done the same. Sadly, those were only the beginning of the injustices. The firm, the colleagues she had trusted and supported with every part of her mind and spirit, had let her down so egregiously that she could scarcely permit the thought without feeling sick to her stomach.

How had she surrounded herself with those so filled with greed and selfishness? She hadn't known these people at all. She laughed. Clearly, she scarcely knew her own sister. What did that say about her?

How had she been so oblivious to the deceit? Her father had once said that her need to see the best in people would be her downfall. Regrettably, his sage words had seen fruition. As difficult a pill as it was to swallow, she had learned a great lesson. She would not be so gullible moving forward.

The silver lining amid all the darkness was that her memories continued to return and she felt far less confused and uncertain. She had reason to believe a great deal of the uncertainty and confusion she had felt in the past several months had been about those around her attempting to hide their treachery. The interference hadn't permitted her mind to properly put the pieces back together.

She could see clearly now.

Clint joined her. "Aren't you cold?"

The breeze had picked up but she'd ignored it. Now that he mentioned it, she shivered. "A little."

"Dinner's ready."

She smiled. "I smelled the ginger and something else, maybe garlic."

"It's one of my favorite entrees from Belinda's." He handed her a glass of wine, and then sipped his own.

"I've heard about that shop. She does gourmet meals for you to take home and heat up at your leisure."

"That's the one."

Natalie sipped her wine. It was fresh and sweet on her tongue, bubbly in her throat. "Thank you for bringing me here. I don't think I could have gone home tonight."

"Sometimes home isn't where we need to be." He leaned forward and braced his forearms on the steel railing. "Sometimes we just need to disappear from all that we know."

"Do you ever do that?" She downed a swallow of wine, needing courage. "Disappear, I mean?" She leaned against the railing.

"Sometimes."

She thought of the elegant home just beyond those disappearing doors that allowed for an unobstructed extension of the main living space onto this amazing terrace. Clint Hayes had an enviable home, a wardrobe that would make the most impeccably dressed man jealous and he was incredibly handsome. Yet, Natalie recognized a sadness in him. Maybe even a little loneliness. She almost laughed out loud at the idea. He could have any woman he desired. His relationship with his detective friends was proof that he possessed the ability to develop and maintain relationships.

"Why are you alone?" Her breath caught. She hadn't meant to say the words.

He straightened, downed the rest of his wine and took the two steps to a table to place his glass there. "The same reason as you, I suppose." He moved back to where she stood frozen, desperate to hear more. "Wouldn't you say?"

He felt so close standing out here with only the city lights and the stars to chase away the darkness. She drained her glass. More courage, she told herself as she placed it next to his. "How can you compare your choices to my reactions to events over which I had no control?"

He waited until she returned to stand next to him. "Your recovery has been nothing short of miraculous. Despite recent events, you've come through amazingly well. So what's stopping you now?"

His deep voice and the intensity in his eyes made her shiver. "Do you mean right now? This very moment?"

"Why not?"

Heat seared through her body. Was he inviting her to be with him? He'd certainly had a different attitude last night. "Is that why you brought me here? I thought—"

He touched her hair. Her voice deserted her as he let his fingers glide through the length of it.

"I don't want to want you." He reached up, traced her lips with the pad of his thumb. "I don't want to lie awake at night thinking about how it would feel to be deep inside you."

Her thighs trembled. "I…don't know what to say."

"Don't say anything." His mouth swooped down and claimed hers. "Let's just do this before I lose my mind."

He picked her up and carried her to his bedroom. He lowered her to her feet, his hands sliding up her torso, drawing her sweater up and off. He stared at her breasts for a long moment before dropping to his knees and removing the sandals she wore. When his fingers unfastened her jeans, she gasped. He leaned forward and kissed her belly button and heat funneled beneath it. The whirlwind was so ferocious she could scarcely breathe.

She sank her fingers into his dark hair, relishing the silky feel. He dragged her jeans down her legs, and she stepped out of them one foot at a time and kicked them aside. He stood and spun her around. His fingers trailed up her spine leaving a path of pure fire in their wake. He unfastened her bra and pushed it off her arms. His lips followed the path of fire he'd ignited, all the way down to her bottom where he teased her relentlessly, tugging down her panties with his teeth. He kissed and licked and tantalized his way back up her legs and then along her spine, taking extra time at her neck. She was burning up, need building so fast she wanted to beg for mercy, but her lips wouldn't form the words.

He turned her around and the instant he took her nipple into his mouth she lost all control. She pushed him away and tugged at the buttons of his shirt. He joined her, tearing at his buttons, pulling loose the shirttail. Her fingers tangled in his fly, slipping loose the button and lowering the zipper. The trousers and the boxer briefs came off in one quick sweep.

He lifted her onto the bed and lowered his body next to hers. She vaguely remembered the last time she'd made love, but this was something far stronger, wilder…soul awakening. He kissed every inch of her, made her come so many times she was certain her mind and body couldn't possibly bear one more moment.

"Please," she pleaded, "I can't take any more."

"Just let go, baby…lose yourself." He trailed his tongue down her belly and lavished her in the most intimate and carnal ways a man could pleasure a woman.

Gasping for breath, she took his advice and threw off all her inhibitions. No rules, no worries, just the incredible pleasure coursing through her veins. Feeling fearless now, she turned the tables on him. She wanted to taste all of him. She wanted to touch him in ways she had never touched anyone. She wanted to drown in the sensation of his voice whispering against her skin… of his body moving against hers.

She wanted him…all of him. And then she wanted more.

Chapter Sixteen

Sunday, September 25, 6:50 a.m.

Clint watched the woman sleeping next to him. He tried to convince himself that last night had been about having ignored his physical needs for far too long, but that wasn't true. He wasn't a fool and he hadn't survived this long by lying to himself.

Last night had been about desire. The basic, naked longing to have something or someone you wanted so desperately. Yes, last night had been about desperation. Complete, utter desperation several degrees above primal craving. He wanted Natalie Drummond for far more than her body. He wanted her mind and spirit. He longed to touch her heart. No…he yearned to own her heart.

More terrifying, he wanted to give himself to her without reservation. This was a place he had never been before. He didn't want to be here now. He wasn't the sort of man she would want to spend her life with.

He freed himself from the tangle of silk sheets and moved away from the bed. The rising sun filtered through the floor-to-ceiling windows, stretching its glow across the white rumpled linens, touching her face. Her long dark hair fanned over her pillow making him want to run his fingers through it. He had learned every part of her…tasted every inch of her. And he wanted more.

His body stirred with need. How easy it would be to slide between those sheets and take her again this morning. She had shown him over and over with her soft whispers and urgent whimpers that she wanted him with equal ferocity. With her touch, her kiss, and the way her body opened and accepted him so completely. The trouble was, he understood that what she had needed—what he had needed—last night was only temporary.

Natalie was in a vulnerable place right now. She was desperate for the truth and equally terrified to trust. He was the anchor she clung to in these turbulent waters. Though she was recovering exceedingly well, the TBI would continue to impact her life on some level. When the case was closed and her life was hers again, she would realize her mistake. She wouldn't look at him the same way and that was the part that terrified him the most.

Clint shook his head. He was a fool. He hit the shower and washed away the evidence of just how big a fool he'd been. He would get his act together and finish the job. He'd never been anything less than completely reliable. He wouldn't fall down on the job now.

CLINT WAS HAVING his second cup of coffee in the morning sun when she found him. She smiled and his chest tightened.

"Coffee's great." She sat down at the table with him and set her cup there. "What a perfect way to spend the morning." She admired the city view. "I love everything about this place."

Despite his best efforts he couldn't help inventorying every detail he adored about her. She had showered and dried her long hair. Though she wore the same sweater and jeans as yesterday, she looked fresh and soft. The urge to carry her back to his bed and block out the rest of the world for a few more days was a palpable force.

"You want breakfast?" Last night they had devoured dinner between lovemaking sessions. Still, he was ravenous this morning. Unfortunately his appetite went well beyond mere food.

She shook her head. "I'm not hungry." She stared at her cup and traced a slow circle around the rim. "I didn't dream last night. At least nothing I remember."

"Is that unusual?" He directed his thoughts to the case. She'd come to him for help and here he was feeling sorry for himself for developing these feelings. Not to mention his selfish need to make love to her again and again.

"In the beginning I took something to help me sleep. It was crucial. My brain seemed to forget when to shut itself down. To heal, it needed rest. When I stopped the sleep aids, the dreams became more vivid and intense. It didn't bother me at first. I was warned that some memories would return that way. You know, hard and fast and complete. Sometimes the dreams were just jumbled pieces of my life. But they were always there, every night. Except last night."

"The wine," he proposed. "I slept like a rock myself."

Her gaze held his, the same desire he felt was crystal clear in those blue depths. "I think it was more than the wine."

"I should get you home." If she stayed and kept looking at him that way he would end up carrying her back to his bed post haste. Not a good idea.

"I called my friend Sadie for an appointment."

"Dr. Morrow?" He searched her face. "Are you feeling all right?" He hadn't thought of anyone but himself last night. He should have realized sex would have a major impact on her emotions for a whole host of reasons.

"Yes." She nodded. "I feel great. Better than I have in a long time."

Now he was confused. "Then why do you need to see your psychologist?"

"I don't want to waste any more time. People are dying. I can't keep waiting for the memories to come back to me. We know Rosen and Vince withheld evidence—or worse. The only witness who can prove what really happened is dead. I must find that evidence. Sadie can help me. She can take me back to the day before the…fall."

"You want to use hypnosis. Have you done that before? Is it safe under the circumstances?" He wasn't comfortable with this. If hypnosis was the answer, surely one of her doctors would have suggested it before now.

"There are always risks when toying with the mind," she confessed. "I'd rather take that risk than to sit around waiting for the next attempt on my life. By now Rosen is aware that I know his secret."

He couldn't have said it better himself, but that didn't mean he liked her plan one bit. He could protect her from outside threats. What she was proposing took her beyond his reach. "We'll talk to Dr. Morrow. If the risk is too great," he shook his head, "we'll find another way."

Natalie scooted back her chair and stood. "I

appreciate your concern, but I've spent the better part of two years having people tell me what's best for me. I think it's time I made a few decisions of my own."

Knowing a brick wall when he hit one, Clint gathered their cups. "You're the boss."

He left the cups in the sink and headed for his closet. He secured his handgun at his belt. Since turning in his badge he rarely carried. With recent events, being armed was warranted. He selected a jacket and a tie. As he secured the silk fabric around his neck, he studied his reflection. At thirty-six he thought his life was on track. Financially secure, a satisfying career, no family obligations other than the occasional call to his mom. Why the abrupt urgent need for more?

He already knew the answer. Everyone he counted as a friend, including his boss, was either getting married or having babies. He wanted that, too.

"Ridiculous." He dismissed the restless feeling and purposely kept his gaze away from the rumpled sheets as he left his bedroom.

Natalie waited near the elevator. She looked him up and down, and then her lips spread into a smile. His gut tightened at the sheer beauty of that smile. His feelings weren't about marriage or having babies—they were about this woman.

Oh yeah. He was in trouble here.

Oxmoor Road
9:40 a.m.

"WE'VE DISCUSSED THIS BEFORE," Natalie insisted. "There's no other way. I have to do it."

Sadie wasn't convinced. "Dr. Cromeans is not a fan of regression therapy. He prefers to allow the memories to return in their own time. Since he's the physician of record on your case, I would need—"

Natalie expected her to resist. "Two people are dead," she reminded her old friend. "There have been at least two, potentially three, attempts on my life. I need to be proactive."

Sadie considered her reasoning for a moment. "You seem more like your old self today. Are you feeling stronger? More confident?"

"Yes." Natalie nodded. "In spite of the trouble cropping up around me, I don't feel out of control." In fact, she felt as if she could take on the world. She felt strong.

"This is very good news, Nat. So many patients who've been through a TBI never fully regain their confidence in self, which is so essential to moving forward with their lives. I am immensely pleased with your progress."

Natalie wanted to tell her about last night, but she couldn't share it just yet. Her pulse reacted to the idea that Clint waited just outside the room.

She had no idea how she would ever convince him to stay once the case was closed. Somehow she would find a way. She didn't want to let him go. The idea might be foolish but her father had taught her to go for what she wanted and to never let go.

She wanted Clint Hayes in her life.

"Do this for me, Sadie," she urged. "I'll sign whatever sort of release is needed. I can't afford not to try and I certainly can't wait another day."

Sadie sighed. "I really wish you would reconsider."

"I won't," Natalie warned. "I have to know where I hid the evidence."

"Though I don't know all the details, I can understand how time is your enemy in this."

Natalie could feel her old friend's resistance weakening. She couldn't make Sadie a target by sharing the tragic truth with her just yet. When this was over and those responsible were brought to justice she would tell her friend everything.

"All right, if you're sure this is what you want."

"I'm sure."

"Let's move to the session seating."

Natalie relocated to the chaise lounge. She sank into the butter-soft leather and closed her eyes.

"Find a comfortable position and just breathe. Deep and slow. Notice how your body relaxes as the air slowly leaves your lungs. Breathe. In…out. Deeper. Slower. Feel how your body is relaxing.

Each breath you release purges your body of the stress and worry. It's going…going…all gone."

Natalie felt so light she could be floating. *Breathe…deep and slow.*

"Imagine you're walking along the street where you live. You can see your house but it's far, far away. As I slowly count you're going closer to home. Each number takes you closer and closer. One…you are so relaxed and your body is just floating toward home. Two…"

Natalie floated along, closer and closer to the home where she'd grown up…where she'd lived her whole life.

"Natalie, it's September eighth two years ago. You wake up that morning feeling relaxed and happy."

Natalie threw the covers back and stepped out of bed. "No," she murmured, fear creeping into her bones.

"It's all right, Natalie, you can see but nothing from that day can hurt you now. Where are you going?"

"I have a meeting at the funeral home with Mrs. Stuart. She has something to show me. She says it's important. I'm worried that it's a setup, but my instincts won't let me ignore her." Natalie's heart started to pound. Her body felt stiff and her lungs burned as if she'd been running.

"I shouldn't go, but I have to. Whoever sent the letters knows something I need to know…"

"Where are you, Natalie?"

Sadie's voice touched her in the darkness like a soothing whisper. Natalie moved toward the sound. She felt calmer now. She could do this. "I have the evidence. I don't know what to do. This is going to change everything." She moved her head side to side. "This is bad…so bad."

"Where are you taking the evidence, Natalie? Do you need to hide it?"

"Yes." In her mind, Natalie opened the pocket doors of her father's study. "It's late. I'll turn it over to the judge in the morning." She needed a safe place to hide it. Natalie searched the room that served as her home office. A really good place where no one would think to look. She went through the drawers and the shelves. Where did she hide it? Her attention landed on the liquor cabinet. "There."

"Where, Natalie?"

"The liquor cabinet." She opened the lower doors and found the beautiful carved wooden case that contained a fifth of Jack Daniels sipping whiskey. It had been a gift to her father from one of his friends. Natalie removed the bottle and set it aside. She carefully folded the two documents and placed them in the box so the bottle would cover them. Then she closed the box and tucked it safely in the farthest corner of the cabinet. "It'll be safe here."

"Where are you going now, Natalie?"

The sound of Sadie's voice was farther and farther away. Natalie stood in the entry hall and gazed up to the second-story landing. It was late. She should get some sleep. Tomorrow she was going to jeopardize her career by doing the right thing. She must be out of her mind. No. No. It was the right thing to do. Poor Mrs. Thompson deserved justice for her family. How could the firm have allowed Rison Medical to get away with what they'd done?

Not fair.

She took the first step up.

"Natalie, you can wake up now."

Sadie's voice was so far away she could hardly hear her. Natalie climbed the stairs and went to her room. She was so tired. She slid into the bed and closed her eyes. She needed to sleep.

"Natalie!"

Natalie opened her eyes. Where was she? At home in bed. What day was it? She had to hurry. She threw back the covers and sat up.

Laugher floated to her.

Whispers brushed her senses. More laughter. April? What was her sister doing here?

Natalie moved into the hall. More whispers, a man's voice this time, drifted in the air. April was in her room with someone. Had she and David come here for some reason? Why didn't they wake her? No, wait. She remembered. April and David had a fight. Had they made up?

What time was it? A single dong sounded downstairs. She wandered in that direction. She reached the landing. Below, the entry hall was dark and yet somehow the grandfather clock stood in a pool of light. *Eleven forty-five.*

Good grief. It wasn't even midnight. She should go back to bed. Her stomach rumbled. Had she forgotten to eat? After the meeting with Mrs. Stuart she'd had no appetite. She could eat now. A sandwich maybe. Coffee would be good. Maybe not. She might not be able to go back to sleep.

"Natalie!"

She frowned. Was that Sadie calling her name? What was she doing here?

Natalie started down the stairs and suddenly her body bowed forward as if something had struck her in the back. She was tumbling down the stairs. Screams surrounded her, rising up in the air until her head slammed into the marble floor.

Darkness.

Whispering voices.

"NATALIE!"

Clint burst into the office. Sadie was shaking Natalie. The screams abruptly stopped and Natalie sat up.

Clint rubbed his neck and swore. "What the hell happened?"

Sadie shook her head. "I'm not sure. She stopped listening to my voice and went off on her own journey. Are you all right, Nat?"

Natalie nodded and then stared at Sadie for a long moment before lifting her gaze to Clint. He held his breath as she spoke. "I know where the evidence is."

Sadie refused to permit them to leave until she was convinced Natalie was calm and feeling balanced. Clint navigated after-church and lunchtime traffic while keeping one eye on his passenger. She hadn't said much since they left her friend's office.

"Did you remember anything else?"

"Just the impact of being pushed...and falling. My head slamming against the floor and then the darkness."

"What about the whispers and the laughter? Could you hear those up till the moment you were pushed?"

She took a few moments to answer. "Yes." She turned to him. "They were still whispering and laughing in April's room."

"I think," Clint said carefully, "in that case we can rule out April and Beckett. If they were still in the bedroom, they were nowhere near you."

"We can also rule out Suzanna and Leonard

and certainly David." She laughed, a sound that held no humor. "April wouldn't have brought her lover to the house if there was a chance David might join them."

"Farago." Maybe Clint just wanted it to be him. He couldn't deny a sense of giddy anticipation at the possibility of seeing the guy go down.

"Or someone he or Rosen hired." She stared out the window. "It's hard to imagine my colleagues as enemies but I know it's true of at least two or three of those closest to me."

He told himself not to do it, but he might as well have been talking to the wall. He placed his hand over hers on the console. "I can't promise this will sharpen your powers of perception to the point you'll never have to worry about being deceived this way again, but I can guarantee you it won't hurt as much next time."

"I suppose that's something."

Clint parked his Audi in her garage. "As soon as we find the documents, we'll take them to the office, make a copy and put them in the safe. We don't want to risk losing the only copy."

"Good idea," Natalie agreed. "I'll call the one attorney in Birmingham I know won't be swayed by the influence of Rosen."

Clint unlocked the door to the kitchen. "Are you sure he's an attorney?"

"He's the best," she assured him.

She smiled and he felt better just seeing those blue eyes sparkle.

Clint stepped ahead of her as they entered the house. He frowned at the idea that they'd failed to set the alarm when they left yesterday. While he surveyed the great room she headed straight to her office. The hair on his neck stood on end. "Natalie, wait."

The doors glided apart with the groan of metal on metal and she hurried in.

"It's about time."

Clint reached for his weapon. Too late. David Keating stood in front of Natalie's desk with a .9 millimeter aimed at her.

"Why don't you close the doors, Mr. Hayes?"

"David, I don't understand. What're you doing?"

Natalie sounded calm but Clint saw the fear in her eyes. He settled his full attention on the man. "Put the gun down and we'll talk about this, Keating."

"I'm not playing games here, Hayes. Do exactly as I say or I will pull this trigger. Take off your jacket," he ordered.

Clint was not giving up his weapon. Grunting and groaning sounded behind them. Someone else was in the room.

"I told you to shut up!" Keating screamed.

Clint couldn't see who was behind them. He didn't dare take his eyes off the bastard with the gun. "Think about what you're doing, Keating. If you hurt her, you won't make it out of here alive. You have my word on that."

"Take off the jacket!" Keating's face was red with fury now.

Clint took his time shrugging off his jacket.

"Toss it on the chair and put your weapon there."

This was it. There would be no going back once he gave up his weapon. Clint met Natalie's gaze, urging her to understand that he had to make a move. She nodded ever so slightly.

Clint tossed his jacket and reached for his weapon.

Keating's attention fixed firmly on him, watching for any sudden moves.

Natalie dropped to the floor.

Keating snapped his attention to her.

Clint fired one shot, aiming for the right shoulder. The bullet hit its target and the weapon dropped from Keating's hand. He howled in pain.

Clint was on him before he had a chance to recover from the shock of being shot. "You okay?" he called to Natalie.

"Yes." She scrambled to her feet.

He slammed Keating down into the nearest chair. Natalie had gone around the desk and was preparing to release Keating's other hostage. *Vince Farago.*

"Leave him," Clint ordered. "We don't know why he's here."

Natalie looked uncertain but she did as Clint said. "Is the duct tape he used on Farago lying around somewhere?"

Natalie grabbed the roll and brought it to him. She grimaced at Keating's continued howling. "I'll call 9-1-1."

"Then call Harper."

While Natalie made the calls, Clint secured Keating, starting with his mouth. "You'll live," he warned. Clint imagined he would wish for death many times before he was out of prison.

Clint left Keating and moved on to the other man. He ripped the duct tape off Farago's mouth, garnering another yelp. "By my estimates you have maybe ten minutes before the police arrive, Farago. Why don't you give me your version of what's going on and maybe I can put in a word for you."

"He came to my house and told me that Natalie wanted to make a deal with us."

"A deal for what?" Clint demanded.

Farago glared at him. "You know what."

Clint glanced over at the liquor cabinet where Natalie was checking for the documents she had hidden there two years ago. She shook her head. Damn it.

"He took them," Farago said.

Clint frowned. "Who took what?"

Keating started making all sorts of grunting and groaning sounds. Natalie tore the tape from his mouth.

"Tell me what you did, David. Tell me now."

"I planted cameras," he said between gasps. "I knew April was having an affair." He glared at Farago. "That bastard paid Beckett to seduce her."

"Beckett said I didn't have to pay him. She wanted him," Farago hurled back.

Clint grabbed the bastard by the chin. "Shut up."

"I saw you," Keating said, his gaze on Natalie. "I was watching from my computer at home and I saw you hide the documents. I heard you talking to him." He glared at Farago. "You told him you had the evidence and you were taking it to the judge the next morning."

"What did any of this have to do with you?" Natalie demanded, fury sparking from her eyes.

"I wanted a political career. I needed leverage to get the kind of backing required. I knew it had to be something big so I drove over here, waited until you were in bed, and came inside. Imagine my surprise when that slut wife of mine showed up with her lover."

Natalie slapped him.

He sneered at her. "I found your evidence and I knew it was my ticket to where I wanted to be.

Art Rosen had the kind of influence I needed. I called Vince and asked him what it was worth."

"Tell her what you did," Farago shouted as sirens sounded outside.

"He told me it wouldn't matter because you were going to the judge and rock the boat. Even without the documentation, you could ruin everything."

"He pushed you down the stairs," Farago shouted.

"And now you'll never have your evidence," Keating said. "All this was for nothing because Stuart can't back you up."

Natalie's face paled.

Clint strode over to Keating, ripped off another length of tape, slapped it over the man's mouth, and then he slammed his fist into his face. Keating's muffled howls made Clint feel just a little better.

"I need that evidence," Natalie said to Clint, the pain in her voice a raw ache inside him.

He turned to Farago. "Actually, I don't think you need it. You have an eye witness to the whole fiasco."

Farago shook his head. "No way. As long as I keep my mouth shut, Rosen will protect me."

Clint walked back to where Farago sat on the floor. He crouched down and looked him straight in the eye. "By the time Keating gets through singing for a plea deal, the firm won't even look at you much less protect you." He leaned even closer. "I was a cop for a long time, Farago. I have contacts in prison. Do I need to spell out how miserable I can make it for you in the tank? You sure you want to take your chances with Rosen?"

"I would listen to him if I were you," Natalie recommended. "Between Keating's testimony and mine, you're screwed, Farago. You and Rosen are going down."

Farago's eyes widened as the sound of sirens grew louder.

"The way I see it," Clint added, "you have one option. Make a deal fast—before Keating. I guarantee you will not like prison."

"How can I be sure my rolling over on Rosen about this case will be enough?" he whined.

"That depends," Clint offered. "Did you kill Imogene Stuart?"

"No! That was Keating!"

Keating made more of those urgent, muffled sounds. Clint ignored him.

Natalie looked even more stricken. "He's right, Vince. You should hurry, otherwise David may get a deal from the DA first."

"Okay, okay! I'll talk to the DA." Farago glanced at Keating. "Right now! I can give him enough to send Rosen away for a very long time." He sneered at Natalie. "While you were busy with all those cream-of-the-crop cases, I was the one doing his dirty work on the cases you never hear about in staff meetings. Call the DA now."

Natalie smiled, the expression weary but triumphant. "I think I can arrange that for you."

It was done. Natalie could have her life back. Clint wanted to feel relieved, to be happy for her. Instead, he felt lost.

Chapter Seventeen

4th Avenue North
Birmingham
Monday, September 26, 5:00 p.m.

The lobby was overflowing. Jess brimmed with pride. The open house had started at two and there had been a steady flow of visitors since. Buddy cut free from the crowd and joined her.

"Looks like we're a success, kid."

Jess gave him a nod. "We are."

The new mayor and every department head at Birmingham PD had passed through this afternoon. Of course, Jess was pretty sure Dan had something to do with that. Her smile widened as she watched him work the crowd. She had been in love with him since she was seventeen years old and he was still the most handsome man she had ever seen. As if to punctuate the thought, the baby kicked. She pressed her hand to her belly and sighed. Life was good.

"Both the new recruits are here," Buddy said. "All we need now are some new cases."

"Those will come," Jess assured him. "There's never a shortage of people who need the kind of help we can offer." Sad but true.

Jess watched the two new hires. Owen Welsh was an excellent choice. Sean Douglas she still had reservations about. He was a far-too-cocky guy. His background as a bodyguard to the stars made his resume desirable, but there was something more than his one failed assignment that nudged at her. Jess couldn't put her finger on it just yet. Before he went out on a case she would know everything about the brazen young man.

"No frowning allowed. Your open house is a smash hit."

She glanced up at Dan and smiled. "I was just thinking."

He leaned down and whispered in her ear. "I was thinking I might take my gorgeous wife home early."

She shivered and tugged on his tie. "Look. Lori and Chet are here. And Sylvia."

Dan groaned. "One more hour and I'm taking you home, Mrs. Burnett."

"Whatever you say, Chief."

Jess glanced around the room. Where were

Clint and Natalie? She'd seen them just a moment ago. Natalie was still stunned that her brother-in-law had committed such atrocities. Jess was rarely surprised by what one human could do to another. All too often the face of evil was one the victim knew too well.

"I swear," Sylvia Baron grabbed Jess and gave her a hug, "if I throw up one more time during an autopsy I'm going to belt my husband."

Jess laughed. "The morning sickness will pass."

Sylvia groaned. "Not soon enough," she grumbled. "Did I tell you Nina is planning Addi's engagement party?"

"You did," Jess said. Nina continued to do exceedingly well on her new medication. Jess could not be happier for the Baron family. Now that she had a child of her own, she understood more so than ever how hard it was to see a child—even an adult child—suffer.

As if another wave of nausea had hit, Sylvia pressed a hand to her belly and made a face. "Why do women do this?"

Jess laughed. She had never seen the medical examiner get even a little queasy at the most gruesome scene. "When the baby arrives you'll understand."

"Who's that gorgeous young man over there?" Sylvia nodded in the direction of Sean Douglas.

"Trouble, I fear."

Sylvia patted her arm. "Nothing you can't handle, I'm confident."

Jess relaxed. Her friend was right. Jess had taken down more than her share of serial killers. A cocky guy like Douglas would be a piece of cake. As if he felt her scrutiny, Douglas's gaze collided with hers. He nodded in that enigmatic way of his.

She would be keeping a close eye on him.

"YOU WANTED TO TALK?" Clint shut the conference room door, closing out the sound of the open house.

Natalie shored up her courage and launched into her practiced speech. "April was such a mess last night, you and I didn't get to talk after the police left."

Her sister had shown up right after the police. David had drugged her coffee. He'd hoped to keep her down for the count until he accomplished his mission. He'd intended to kill Natalie and Clint and then Vince, staging the scene as if Vince had committed the murders and been mortally wounded in the process. David had even coerced Vince into picking him up so no one would see his car at the house. Her brother-in-law had been that greedy for power.

David had been one of those unexpected faces

of evil Jess Burnett had told her about. Eventually the wounds he'd caused would heal.

"What do you want to talk about?" Clint asked, nudging Natalie from the troubling thoughts.

She smiled. "I wanted to thank you for all you did. I wouldn't have been able to do this without you. Mrs. Thompson and her family will finally have the vindication they deserve."

"No thanks necessary. I provided a service. You paid the fee."

He wanted to sound indifferent but she knew he didn't feel that way. And she was not going to let him pretend nothing had happened between them. "Actually, I was interested in an additional service."

His gaze narrowed. "I don't want to play games with you, Natalie."

With a deep breath, she took the leap. She put her arms around him and stared deeply into those dark eyes. "I want to explore the feelings I have for you. The feelings," she said when he would have loosened her grip on him, "I know you feel, too."

"I'm not the right man for you."

"You're the only man for me." She went up on tiptoe and pressed her lips to his. He resisted at first, but then he surrendered. And then he took control of the kiss.

"I'm not what you need," he murmured against her lips.

"You're everything I want," she whispered back. "And more."

His fingers threaded into her hair and he kissed her for so long her knees went weak. "Fair warning, once you're mine, I won't let you go."

"I'm counting on it," she whispered.

He flashed her a grin before lowering his lips to hers. Despite all the things she wanted to say about the wonderful future they were going to have together, Natalie lost herself to the promise of his kiss.

They had the rest of their lives and she would never take a single moment of it for granted.

* * * * *

Look for the next FACES OF EVIL *title,*
STILL WATERS, coming next month
from Debra Webb and Harlequin Intrigue!
Read on for an excerpt!

Chapter One

4th Avenue North
Birmingham, Alabama
Monday, October 17, 9:30 a.m.

Jess Harris Burnett had just poured her third cup of decaf when the jingle of the bell over the door sounded. As she walked toward the lobby, she heard receptionist Rebecca Scott welcoming the visitor to B&C Investigations. The office had been open almost a month now. Jess and her lifelong friend Buddy Corlew had made a good decision going into business together. With a nineteen-month-old daughter and a son due in a mere six weeks—Jess rubbed her enormous belly—stepping away from her position as deputy chief of Birmingham's major-crimes team had been the right move.

The memory of being held prisoner by Ted Holmes attempted to bully into her thoughts and

Jess pushed it away. Holmes, like the many serial killers before him she had helped to track down, was history now. Still, Jess was well aware that there would always be a new face of evil just around the next corner. She intended to leave tracking down the killers to the Birmingham PD. Her goal now was to concentrate on the victims. With B&C Investigations, she was accomplishing that goal.

"I'll let Mrs. Burnett know you're here, Ms. Coleman," Rebecca was saying as Jess came into the lobby.

"Gina, what brings you by this morning?" Jess flashed a smile for the receptionist. "Thank you, Rebecca. We'll be in my office."

Gina Coleman, Birmingham's beloved and award-winning television journalist, gave Jess a hug. "You look great!"

"You're the one who looks great," Jess countered. "Married life agrees with you."

Gina smiled and gave Jess another quick hug. On the way to her office, Jess grabbed her coffee and offered her friend a cup.

"No thanks. I've had way too much already this morning."

When they were settled in Jess's office, Gina surveyed the small space. "You've done a wonderful job of making this place comfortable."

Jess was proud of how their offices had turned

out. The downtown location was good for business even if the building was a very old one. In Jess's opinion, the exposed-brick walls gave the place character. It was a good fit. Most anyone who knew them would say that she and Buddy had more than a little character.

"Thanks." Jess sipped her decaf and smiled. "You really do seem happy." Gina looked amazing, as always. Her long brunette hair and runway-model looks had ensured her a position in the world of television news, but it was her incredible ability to find the story that had made her an award-winning, highly sought-after journalist. Her personal bravery, too, inspired Jess. Gina had taken some fire when she'd announced she was gay and married the woman she loved. Standing firm, Gina had weathered the storm.

"I am very happy." Gina stared at her hands a moment. When she met Jess's gaze once more, her face was clouded with worry. "Barb and I need your help."

"What can I do? Name it." Jess set her coffee aside.

"A couple of hours ago, Barb's younger sister, Amber, was called into the BPD about a murder."

Jess could feel a frown lining her brow, reminding her that by the time this baby was in high school, she would look like his grandmother rather than his mother. She spotted a new wrinkle every time she looked in the mirror. *Don't even go there.*

"I hadn't heard. There was a homicide last night?" This time a year ago, Jess would have known the persons of interest and the prime suspects in every homicide long before an arrest was made in the city of Birmingham. Not anymore. Dan made it a point not to discuss work when he came home. Though she could still nudge him for details when the need arose; it was one of the perks of being married to the chief of police. A sense of well-being warmed her when she thought of her husband. He was a genuinely good man.

"Dan explained as much as he was at liberty to share. He assured me it was routine questioning, but I'm worried. I told him I was coming to you." Gina sighed. "I don't think he was very happy about my decision. He obviously prefers to keep murder and mayhem away from the mother of his children."

Two years ago, Jess would have been jealous at hearing Gina had spoken to Dan. The two had once been an on-again, off-again item. Now she counted Gina as a good friend. "Don't worry about Dan." Jess shook her head. "I've warned him time and again that just because I'm no longer a cop doesn't mean I won't be investigating murders."

"If he had his way, you'd retire," Gina teased. "We both know how he feels about keeping you safe."

Jess had been cursed with more than her fair share of obsessed killers during her career, first as an FBI profiler and then as a deputy chief in Birmingham PD. Dan's concern was understandable if unnecessary. Just because she was a mother now didn't mean she couldn't take care of herself. Admittedly, she had grown considerably more cautious.

"Tell me about the case." Considering it was a murder case, she could get the details from Lieutenant Chet Harper or Sergeant Lori Wells. Chet had recently been named acting chief of the small major crimes team Jess had started, SPU, and Lori had been reassigned to Crimes Against Persons. One or the other would be investigating the homicide case. Jess hoped the case was with Harper. She counted Lori as her best friend, but the new chief of Crimes Against Persons Division, Captain Vanessa Aldridge, was brash, obstinate and carried the biggest chip on her shoulder Jess had ever encountered.

Though they'd only met once or twice, Jess was familiar with Barbara's younger sister. Amber Roberts was a reporter at Channel Six, the same station as Gina. She was young, beautiful and talented. Amber and Barbara's parents were from old money, but Gina would be the first to attest to the fact that a sparkling pedigree didn't exempt a person from murder. Gina's own sister had paid the price for her part in a long-ago tragedy.

"Kyle Adler's body was found in his home yesterday. He'd been stabbed repeatedly. Amber hardly knew the man. The very notion is ludicrous." Gina held up a hand. "I know you're probably thinking that I felt the same way about Julie, but this is different. Amber had nothing to do with this man's murder."

As much as Jess sympathized with Gina, Amber would not have been questioned if the police hadn't found some sort of connection between her and the victim. "The police have something," she reminded her friend. "You know this. What about the murder weapon? Was it found?"

"No, they haven't found the murder weapon." Gina shook her head. "The whole thing is insane. Amber swears the only time she ever saw this guy was when he made a delivery to her or someone at the station. Apparently, he made a living delivering for various shops around town. But the cops claim they found evidence indicating she'd been in his house. Unless someone is framing her, it simply isn't possible."

Jess chewed her bottom lip a moment. "It's conceivable someone may have wanted Adler dead and set it up to look as though another person, like Amber, committed the act."

"If that's true—" Gina leaned forward "—not only do we need help finding the actual murderer, whom the police may not even try to find, we also need to protect Amber. She could be in danger from the real killer."

Jess sent a text to Harper. "Let's see who's working the case first, then we'll know whether or not we have to worry about finding the truth. As for the other, I agree—if Amber is being framed, it's quite possible she could be in danger. Personal security would be a wise step until we know what we're dealing with."

"Buddy said you do protective services as well as private investigations."

"We do," Jess agreed. "Right now the only investigator we have available is Sean Douglas."

Gina's gaze narrowed. "I'm sensing some hesitation. Do you have reservations as to whether he can handle the job?"

Jess considered how to answer the question. "He spent the past five years as a bodyguard to various celebrities in Hollywood." She shrugged. "Based on our research into his background, he was very, very good at his job. For two years prior to that, he was a cop with the LAPD. He's had all the right training and his references are impeccable."

Gina said, "There's a *but* coming."

"His last assignment was Lacy James."

Gina sat back in her chair. "Jesus."

Lacy James had been a rising pop star. The rumors about drug abuse had followed her from singing in the church choir in her hometown of Memphis all the way to her Grammy nomination in LA last year.

"Her agent hired Douglas to keep an eye on her," Jess explained. "According to Douglas, she had been straight for a while and her agent wanted to ensure she stayed that way. Six months into the assignment, she died of an overdose."

"Damn." Gina pressed her hands to her face, then took a breath. "Do you think what happened was in some way his fault?"

Jess shook her head. "Responsibility for what happened to Lacy James lies with her agent and her other handlers. They cared more about her career than they did her health and welfare. My only hesitation is that Douglas is a little too cocky for his own good. I think he uses attitude to cover the pain and guilt he feels about James's death." Jess paused to weigh her words. "I'm concerned his need to prove himself again might be an issue, but as for his ability to protect a client, he's more than capable."

Gina's expression brightened. "Trust me, whatever this guy's attitude, Amber can handle it. You don't rise as rapidly in my business as she has without a tough skin and a little attitude. I'm desperate, Jess. I promised Barb I would take care of this."

Jess felt confident Gina was right about Amber. Putting herself in front of the camera every day was not only hard work, it wasn't for the faint of heart. "Why don't I learn all I can from the BPD and then I'll brief Douglas. I'll arrange a meeting with Amber and we'll go from there."

"I will be forever in your debt."

"We'll take care of Amber," Jess assured her friend.

Gina stood. Jess did the same, albeit a little less gracefully.

"I'm aware that we don't always know a person as well as we believe—even the people closest to us," Gina confessed, "but I would wager all I own that Amber had nothing to do with this man's death."

Jess nodded resolutely. "Then all we need to do is ensure she stays safe until the BPD can find his killer."

Chapter Two

Forest Brook Drive, Homewood, 12:32 p.m.

Amber Roberts entered the necessary code to stop the infernal beeping of her security system, tossed her keys on the table by the door, then kicked off her heels. This had been the longest morning of her life. She closed her eyes and reminded herself to breathe as the man assigned to keep an eye on her rushed past to have a look before she went any farther into the house.

Forcing her mind and body to focus on her normal routine, she locked the front door and set the alarm. Without waiting to hear the all-clear signal, she grabbed her shoes and headed for her bedroom. This was her home. The alarm had still been set, for God's sake. If anyone was in her house, he or she had been here since Amber left this morning. Otherwise, the alarm would have gone off, right? She closed her eyes again. At this point she wasn't sure of anything.

Her stomach knotted at the memory of the police showing up just as her early-morning news broadcast ended. Everyone had watched as the detective explained she was needed downtown and then escorted her from the station. She didn't have to look to know her face would be plastered over the evening papers as well as the internet and television broadcasts.

The damage control had to start now. She'd already tweeted and posted on Instagram and Facebook. The station had backed her up, as well. If the reaction didn't make her sound petty and paranoid, she would swear Gerard Stevens from the station's primary competitor had set her up.

Amber walked into her closet and shoved her shoes into their slots. Her head spun as she dragged off the dress that would forever remind her of the interview room where she'd endured a relentless interrogation by one of the BPD's finest. She tossed the dress into the dry-cleaning hamper and reached for a pair of sweatpants and a T-shirt. Worst of all, a man was dead. Though she'd only known him in passing, she felt bad about his murder. He was someone's son. Probably someone's brother and significant other. She pulled on the sweatpants. Most people had a life—unlike her. Gina and Barb warned her repeatedly that she was going to be sorry for allowing her life to fly by while she was totally absorbed by work.

Who had time for a social life? Gina should know better than anyone. Amber was fairly confident her mentor was saying what Barb expected her to say. It didn't matter either way. Amber was twenty-eight; her top priority was her career. She still had decades for falling in love and building a family.

Even if her narrow focus on her career did get lonely sometimes.

She yanked on the T-shirt and kicked the thought aside. The police believed she was somehow involved in a man's murder. Her love life, or lack thereof, was the least of her worries.

How the hell the police could think she was involved was the million-dollar question. Why in the world would she hurt this man, much less kill him? She scarcely knew him. He had made a few deliveries to her house and at the station. He was always pleasant, but they never exchanged more than a dozen words. None of what she'd been told by the police so far made the slightest bit of sense.

"The house is clear."

Amber jumped, slamming her elbow into the wall. Frowning at the broad-shouldered man filling the doorway to her closet, she rubbed her funny bone.

"Thank you," she said, though she didn't quite feel thankful. She did not want a babysitter. She hadn't killed anyone and there was no reason for a soul to want to harm her. Reporting the news for the past six-plus years had given her certain insights into situations like this one, and hiring a bodyguard this early in the investigation was overreacting. There could only be two potential explanations for her current dilemma: mistaken identity or a frame job. Both happened. As hard as she tried, she could come up with no other explanations.

Her bodyguard's gaze roamed from her face all the way to her toes and back with a couple of unnecessary pauses in between. Now, that annoyed her. He was here to keep her safe—supposedly. He had no business looking at her as if she were the next conquest on his radar. Though she suspected Mr. Sexy-As-Hell usually didn't have to work very hard to get what he wanted. The man was gorgeous. Tall, with those broad shoulders that narrowed into a lean waist. Thick blond hair just the right length for threading your fingers through and deep blue eyes. His muscular build attested to his dedicated workout ethics. With every extra thump of her pulse, she understood that beneath his smooth, tanned skin

was an ego large enough for the Iron Man that
watched over the city of Birmingham from high
atop Red Mountain.

Sean Douglas was hot and he damn well knew
it.

As if he agreed wholeheartedly with her assessment, he gifted her with a nod and disappeared.

Amber sighed. She should pull herself together.
Her attorney, Frank Teller, was on his way over
with whatever details the police had shared with
him. They'd done nothing but ask questions this
morning. Each time her attorney had asked about
the evidence, the detective had evaded the question. Still, she hadn't needed a lawyer to tell her
that she wouldn't have been called in and so thoroughly questioned had there been no evidence.
Friends, colleagues and people acquainted with
the victim were questioned in their homes or
workplaces. Only the ones about to be named a
person of interest—or worse, a suspect—were
hauled to the station and interviewed. The police had wanted her off balance—which was not
a good thing.

How the hell was this possible?

What she needed was a couple of cocktails and
a good night's sleep. Maybe she'd wake up in the
morning and discover this had all been just one
big old nightmare.

Finding Sean Douglas kicked back on the sofa in her living room reminded her that the situation was all too real.

"I put on a pot of coffee." He leaned forward and braced his forearms on his knees. "I figured some caffeine would be useful in the next few hours."

She would have preferred a pumpkin-spice latte, but she'd been too emotional to think of dropping by her favorite coffee shop after leaving the police department. Her parents were beside themselves. They were in a remote part of Africa on a medical-aid mission and couldn't get back for days. She and her sister, Barbara, had insisted their parents stay and do the important work they'd gone there to do. This entire business was nothing more than a mistake. Surely it would be cleared up in a day or two.

Belatedly she remembered to say "Thank you." Frank Teller was a coffee drinker. Vaguely, she wondered how Douglas had known this or if he was a coffee guy, too.

"I can call in some lunch for delivery. I'm guessing you didn't take time for breakfast this morning."

She appreciated the offer, but said, "I had a protein drink. I'm fine."

He dismissed her response with a wave of his hand. "How about pizza or Chinese? Your choice."

She couldn't possibly eat. "I'm not hungry. Feel free to raid my kitchen or order something for yourself."

His mouth eased into a lopsided grin. "Already done that. You're fresh out of real food."

A frown furrowed her brow. He'd prowled through her kitchen? What kind of bodyguard checked the fridge?

"Why don't you tell me about yourself," he suggested with a pat of the sofa cushion next to him.

Amber felt sure that inviting pat worked well for him under normal circumstances, but those blue eyes and that hopeful smile did little other than annoy her at the moment. "Weren't you briefed on my case?"

The need for personal security was entirely new to her, but instinct told her a man assigned to protect her would certainly have been briefed about the situation. Small talk was the furthest thing from her mind. He needed to find a way to entertain himself if he was bored. She had no desire to chat.

"I was." He clasped his hands between his spread thighs.

"What else do you need to know?" She gave herself a mental pat on the back for not sounding as snippy as she felt.

"Until this situation is resolved," he began,

tracking her movements with those blue eyes as she settled in a chair a few feet away, "we'll be spending a lot of time together. It's helpful to know a little more than the facts of the case. What time do you like to get up in the mornings? What's your usual bedtime? Do you watch television or read or just relax in the evenings? Should I expect company? Is there a boyfriend to accommodate?" He shrugged. "Things like that are good to know."

For the love of Mike. Amber shook off the frustration. His request had merit. *No need to be unreasonable.* "I'm up at six unless I'm called to a scene earlier or I host the morning news, the way I did this morning. I go to bed right after the ten-o'clock news, assuming I haven't been called out to a scene. I usually leave the television turned on all night." She glanced at the dark screen hanging on the wall above her fireplace. She imagined that every channel was running stories about her and the murder. "I might be taking a break from that habit for a few days."

"Understandable." He cocked an eyebrow. "What about the boyfriend?"

"There is no boyfriend." Somehow saying it out loud sounded far worse than simply knowing it. She hadn't been in a serious relationship in over a year. Maybe there wouldn't be another one. Who had time? More important, who cared?

She had everything she needed. *If that's so, why the sudden need to justify your status?*

He made a knowing sound as something like surprise flashed across his face. "A girlfriend, then?"

The assumption was a reasonable one, she supposed, considering her sister, Barbara, was in a same-sex relationship. "No girlfriend."

He made one of those male grunts that could convey surprise as easily as indifference. Either way, the sound got on her already-frazzled nerves.

"Your degree is in mass communications," he said, changing the subject. "When did you decide you preferred working in front of the camera versus behind it?"

"I didn't decide. The journalist I assisted during my first assignment was in a car accident. Everyone was on the scene except her, and the cameraman told me to get in front of the camera and do the job. The audience responded well to me, so that's where the powers that be decided I should be."

"But you had aspirations?"

Amber nodded. "I had my heart set on hosting one of the big entertainment news shows." She laughed, remembering the horror on her parents' faces when she'd told them. "It wasn't exactly the career my family had hoped for."

He smiled. It was nice. Really nice. Too nice, damn it. "Your parents and your sister are all doctors."

"Yes. I'm the black sheep." The realization that her words had never been truer stole the air from her lungs. Now she was a potential suspect in a homicide.

The doorbell saved her from going down that pity path. She stood to go to the door, but Douglas moved ahead of her and checked the security viewfinder.

"It's Mr. Teller."

Douglas opened the door and Teller came inside. He'd already been introduced to the man who would be keeping watch over her. There was just something wrong with calling him a bodyguard. Particularly since she continued to have a bit of trouble keeping her attention off his body. The foolish reaction had to be about sex. She hadn't been intimate with anyone since she and Josh ended their relationship. Good grief, had it been an entire year?

Her gaze drifted to the man assigned to protect her. *Don't even go there.*

"We should speak privately," Frank Teller announced before saying hello. He looked from Amber to Douglas and back.

"Whatever you have to say," Amber countered, "I'd like him to hear it, as well." In all likelihood,

she'd have to fill him and his boss in later anyway. Why pretend any aspect of this could be
kept private?

When Teller relented, Douglas insisted on
serving the coffee. Amber was happy to let him
do the honors. Her knees were feeling a little
weak as she sank back into her chair. Maybe it
was the grim expression Teller wore.

He placed his briefcase on the coffee table and
opened it. "The news is not good."

Amber's stomach did the sinking now. "What
sort of evidence could they possibly have? I don't
even know this man! He…he made deliveries
to my house and the station a couple of times."
Maybe more than a couple of times. Still, the
whole thing was ludicrous.

"Amber—" Teller closed his briefcase and
placed the folder he'd removed atop it "—I've
known your family for most of my life. Your
father is my father's personal physician. Your
mother was my pediatrician. I, of all people,
know this is wrong somehow. You couldn't possibly have harmed this man. Yet, the evidence is
enough to make even me have second thoughts."

The trembling that had started this morning
after the initial shock that no one was playing a
joke on her started anew. The police had mentioned evidence without providing the details.
"What evidence? I don't know how they could

find evidence that leads back to me in a home where I've never been...on a body I've never touched."

"They found a teacup with your prints on it."

"What?" The situation had just gone from unbelievable to incomprehensible. "If there is anything in that poor man's house that either belonged to me or bore my prints, someone—besides me—put it there."

Before Teller could respond, Douglas returned with the coffee. He'd gone to the trouble to find her grandmother's serving tray and to dig out the china cups and saucers rather than the stoneware mugs. He'd even prepared the creamer and sugar servers. Her disbelief was temporarily sidelined by the idea that he would think to go to so much trouble.

Douglas placed the tray on the coffee table and she noted there were only two cups. "If you need me for anything—" he hitched his thumb toward the rear of the house "—I'll be outside checking the perimeter."

"Thank you." Amber suddenly didn't want anyone else to hear these incredible lies—at least not until she had heard them.

When Douglas was gone, Teller said, "Amber, I realize this is shocking."

He'd certainly nailed her feelings with that statement. "I don't understand how any of this happened." She shook her head, overwhelmed and confused and, honestly, terrified. "You see it on television or in the movies, but this is real life. My life."

"Do you drink a tea called Paradise Peach?"

Something cold and dark welled inside her. She moistened her lips and cleared her throat. "Yes. It's my favorite. There's a specialty shop downtown that stocks it."

"A can of Paradise Peach tea was found in the victim's home. Your prints were on the can."

Worry furrowed her brow and bumped her pulse rate to a faster rhythm. "Maybe he shopped there, too. He may have picked up a can after I did." Hope knotted in her chest, but it was short-lived. How did a person prove a theory as full of circumstantial holes as the one she'd just suggested?

"Certainly," he agreed. "Bear in mind that the burden of proof is not ours. It will be up to the BPD to prove their case. For that they need evidence, which brings us to the cup that also bore your prints."

The rationale she had attempted to use earlier vanished. Sweet Jesus, she felt as if she had just awakened in the middle of a horror film and she was the next victim. All she had to do now was scream.

"Take a look at these crime-scene photos." He

opened the folder and removed two eight-by-ten photographs. He scooted his briefcase and the serving platter to the far side of the table and placed the photographs in front of her. "These are copies, so they're not the best quality."

The first one showed the victim lying on the floor next to the dining table in what she presumed was his kitchen. Blood had soaked his shirt. He appeared to have multiple stab wounds to the chest. Poor man. She swallowed back the lump of emotion that rose in her throat and moved on to the second one. The second was a wider-angle view showing more of the room. Definitely the kitchen. Her attention zeroed in on the table. The table was set for two. Teacups sat in saucers, each flanked by a spoon and linen napkin. She squinted at the pattern on the cups. A floral pattern for sure, but difficult to distinguish.

"He was having tea with someone." She lifted her gaze to Teller's. "Whoever that person was, he or she is likely the one who killed him.

"Based on the prints found at the scene, the police believe that person was you."

Hands shaking, she pressed her fingers to her mouth to hold back the cry of outrage. "The medical examiner is certain about the time of death?"

Teller nodded. "Last Friday night, around eight o'clock. It'll be a while before we have the autopsy results, which will tell us what he had for dinner and various other details that may or may not help our case."

Amber made a face. "How is what he had for dinner relevant?"

"Knowing what and where he ate might help our case," Teller explained. "The police might be able to track down the restaurant—if he ate out—and someone there might remember if he was alone."

Sounded like a long shot to her. The detectives had pressed her over and over about her whereabouts on Friday night. It was the one Friday night in recent history that she'd come home early and hit the sack. She hadn't spent any time doing research at the station, she hadn't spoken to anyone, and she'd had no company. None of her neighbors could confirm she was home. She hadn't done any work on her home computer, which might have confirmed her whereabouts. Bottom line, she had no alibi.

Disgusted, she shook her head. "Single people all over the world should be terrified of spending a quiet evening at home alone." If she were married or involved in a relationship, she might have spent time or at least spoken to her plus-one that evening.

"There's more."

His somber tone caused her heart to skip a beat.

"A pair of panties were found in his bed. There

was trace evidence. A pubic hair and a much longer hair…" He touched his head. "They want you to agree to a DNA test."

The heart that had stumbled a moment ago slammed against her ribs now. "Do you think I should?" She shrugged. Considering her fingerprints were there, she couldn't help but feel somewhat tentative as to how to proceed. "I know I haven't been in his house or his bed, so I have nothing to hide, but my fingerprints were there." She pressed a hand to her throat. "If someone is setting me up…"

He reached into his folder and removed another photograph. "Do you recognize these?"

The red panties in the photograph stole her ability to draw in air. She shot to her feet and rushed to her bedroom. Opening drawer after drawer, she rifled through her things and then slammed each one closed in turn. Her pulse pounding, she moved to the laundry hamper.

The panties weren't there.

Teller stood at her bedroom door, worry lining his face. "Lots of women have red panties. My wife has red panties. How can you be sure you recognize these?"

Her lungs finally filled with air. "The little bows." She paused to release the big breath she'd managed to draw in. "There should be a little satin red bow on each side. One is missing. It annoys me every time I see it. I've meant to throw them away and keep forgetting."

Of course, any woman with red panties that sported little red bows could be missing one of those bows. In her gut, Amber knew better than to believe it was a mere coincidence. Her red one-bowed panties were gone. There was a teacup in the man's house, for God's sake, with her prints on it. She didn't need a DNA test to prove a damned thing. The hair and any other trace evidence would be hers, as well. Whoever wanted to make her appear guilty had done a bang-up job.

Douglas appeared behind Teller. "Is everything okay?"

No. Everything was not okay. In fact, nothing was okay.

"I'll do the DNA test," Amber said to the man representing her.

Teller gave her a resigned nod. "I'll set it up."

Dear God. She was in serious trouble here.

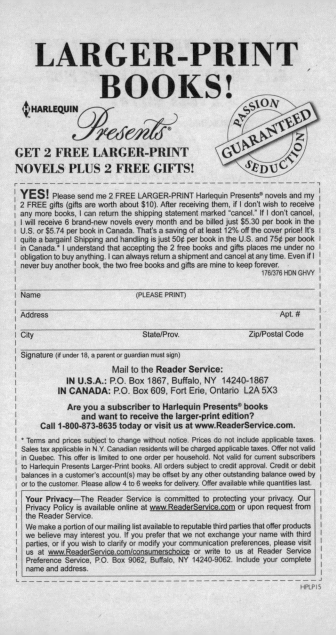

LARGER-PRINT BOOKS!

H HARLEQUIN

Presents®

GET 2 FREE LARGER-PRINT NOVELS PLUS 2 FREE GIFTS!

PASSION GUARANTEED SEDUCTION

YES! Please send me 2 FREE LARGER-PRINT Harlequin Presents® novels and my 2 FREE gifts (gifts are worth about $10). After receiving them, if I don't wish to receive any more books, I can return the shipping statement marked "cancel." If I don't cancel, I will receive 6 brand-new novels every month and be billed just $5.30 per book in the U.S. or $5.74 per book in Canada. That's a saving of at least 12% off the cover price! It's quite a bargain! Shipping and handling is just 50¢ per book in the U.S. and 75¢ per book in Canada.* I understand that accepting the 2 free books and gifts places me under no obligation to buy anything. I can always return a shipment and cancel at any time. Even if I never buy another book, the two free books and gifts are mine to keep forever.

176/376 HDN GHVY

Name _____ (PLEASE PRINT) _____

Address _____ Apt. # _____

City _____ State/Prov. _____ Zip/Postal Code _____

Signature (if under 18, a parent or guardian must sign) _____

Mail to the **Reader Service:**
IN U.S.A.: P.O. Box 1867, Buffalo, NY 14240-1867
IN CANADA: P.O. Box 609, Fort Erie, Ontario L2A 5X3

**Are you a subscriber to Harlequin Presents® books
and want to receive the larger-print edition?
Call 1-800-873-8635 today or visit us at www.ReaderService.com.**

* Terms and prices subject to change without notice. Prices do not include applicable taxes. Sales tax applicable in N.Y. Canadian residents will be charged applicable taxes. Offer not valid in Quebec. This offer is limited to one order per household. Not valid for current subscribers to Harlequin Presents Larger-Print books. All orders subject to credit approval. Credit or debit balances in a customer's account(s) may be offset by any other outstanding balance owed by or to the customer. Please allow 4 to 6 weeks for delivery. Offer available while quantities last.

Your Privacy—The Reader Service is committed to protecting your privacy. Our Privacy Policy is available online at www.ReaderService.com or upon request from the Reader Service.

We make a portion of our mailing list available to reputable third parties that offer products we believe may interest you. If you prefer that we not exchange your name with third parties, or if you wish to clarify or modify your communication preferences, please visit us at www.ReaderService.com/consumerschoice or write to us at Reader Service Preference Service, P.O. Box 9062, Buffalo, NY 14240-9062. Include your complete name and address.

HPLP15

LARGER-PRINT BOOKS!
GET 2 FREE LARGER-PRINT NOVELS PLUS
2 FREE GIFTS!

HARLEQUIN®

Romance

From the Heart, For the Heart

YES! Please send me 2 FREE LARGER-PRINT Harlequin® Romance novels and my 2 FREE gifts (gifts are worth about $10). After receiving them, if I don't wish to receive any more books, I can return the shipping statement marked "cancel." If I don't cancel, I will receive 4 brand-new novels every month and be billed just $5.09 per book in the U.S. or $5.49 per book in Canada. That's a savings of at least 15% off the cover price! It's quite a bargain! Shipping and handling is just 50¢ per book in the U.S. and 75¢ per book in Canada.* I understand that accepting the 2 free books and gifts places me under no obligation to buy anything. I can always return a shipment and cancel at any time. Even if I never buy another book, the two free books and gifts are mine to keep forever.

119/319 HDN GHWC

Name	(PLEASE PRINT)

Address	Apt. #

City	State/Prov.	Zip/Postal Code

Signature (if under 18, a parent or guardian must sign)

Mail to the **Reader Service:**
IN U.S.A.: P.O. Box 1867, Buffalo, NY 14240-1867
IN CANADA: P.O. Box 609, Fort Erie, Ontario L2A 5X3
Want to try two free books from another line?
Call 1-800-873-8635 or visit www.ReaderService.com.

* Terms and prices subject to change without notice. Prices do not include applicable taxes. Sales tax applicable in N.Y. Canadian residents will be charged applicable taxes. Offer not valid in Quebec. This offer is limited to one order per household. Not valid for current subscribers to Harlequin Romance Larger-Print books. All orders subject to credit approval. Credit or debit balances in a customer's account(s) may be offset by any other outstanding balance owed by or to the customer. Please allow 4 to 6 weeks for delivery. Offer available while quantities last.

Your Privacy—The Reader Service is committed to protecting your privacy. Our Privacy Policy is available online at www.ReaderService.com or upon request from the Reader Service.

We make a portion of our mailing list available to reputable third parties that offer products we believe may interest you. If you prefer that we not exchange your name with third parties, or if you wish to clarify or modify your communication preferences, please visit us at www.ReaderService.com/consumerschoice or write to us at Reader Service Preference Service, P.O. Box 9062, Buffalo, NY 14240-9062. Include your complete name and address.

HRLP15

LARGER-PRINT BOOKS!
GET 2 FREE LARGER-PRINT NOVELS PLUS
2 FREE GIFTS!

❖ HARLEQUIN®

super romance®

More Story...More Romance

> # WESTERN WP PROMISES

YES! Please send me **The Western Promises Collection** in Larger Print. This collection begins with 3 FREE books and 2 FREE gifts (gifts valued at approx. $14.00 retail) in the first shipment, along with the other first 4 books from the collection! If I do not cancel, I will receive 8 monthly shipments until I have the entire 51-book Western Promises collection. I will receive 2 or 3 FREE books in each shipment and I will pay just $4.99 US/ $5.89 CDN for each of the other four books in each shipment, plus $2.99 for shipping and handling per shipment. *If I decide to keep the entire collection, I'll have paid for only 32 books, because 19 books are FREE! I understand that accepting the 3 free books and gifts places me under no obligation to buy anything. I can always return a shipment and cancel at any time. My free books and gifts are mine to keep no matter what I decide.

272 HCN 3070 472 HCN 3070

Name	(PLEASE PRINT)

Address	Apt. #

City	State/Prov.	Zip/Postal Code

Signature (if under 18, a parent or guardian must sign)

Mail to the **Reader Service**:
IN U.S.A.: P.O. Box 1867, Buffalo, NY 14240-1867
IN CANADA: P.O. Box 609, Fort Erie, Ontario L2A 5X3